# Manor of Secrets

## Also by Katherine Longshore

*Gilt*

*Tarnish*

*Brazen*

# Manor of Secrets

Katherine Longshore

Point

Library of Congress Cataloging-in-Publication Data

Longshore, Katherine.
Manor of secrets / by Katherine Longshore. — First edition.
pages cm
Summary: Beautiful, wealthy, and sheltered Lady Charlotte Edmonds, sixteen, and hardworking, clever kitchen maid Janie Seward are both ready for change, and as their paths overlap in The Manor, rules are broken and secrets revealed that will alter the course of their lives forever.
ISBN 978-0-545-56758-9
[1. Social classes — Fiction. 2. Secrets — Fiction. 3. Identity — Fiction. 4. England — Social conditions — 19th century — Fiction. 5. Great Britain — History — 19th century — Fiction.] I. Title.
PZ7.L864Man 2014
[Fic] — dc23
2013019246

12 11 10 9 8 7 6 5 4 3 2 1 14 15 16 17 18/0

Printed in the U.S.A. 23
First edition, February 2014
Book design by Yaffa Jaskoll

To Freddie and Charlie, who make every day an adventure and are always worth the risk

# Chapter I

*Adventure awaits.*

Charlotte Edmonds stood on the patio and looked out across the wide expanse of lawn. The canopy glowed flat white against a backdrop of trees, surrounded by men in linen jackets and women in pastel silks and floaty chiffons. Like ants at a picnic, milling and gossiping and picking at bits of food. Perfectly content.

But hardly an adventure.

Charlotte fidgeted with the buttons on her gloves, avoiding eye contact with her mother. Lady Diane sat on a chaise in the shade of an ancient oak. Her blonde hair didn't show a hint of gray, and her slate-colored and severely tailored day dress only served to heighten the steel of her eyes. The space beside her yawned empty, waiting for Charlotte to fill it.

Expectation of Charlotte's every future move laid out in pale silk and small talk.

The thought made Charlotte want to run. Across the terrace, over the ha-ha, and into the trees beyond. Never to look back.

But the ha-ha lay at the far end of the lawn, and she'd have to dodge neighbors, footmen, and her mother to get there. And then dive the four feet to the pasture below. Her bid for freedom would surely result in broken bones and a near-terminal decline in social standing. Her mother would scarcely give her time to heal before packing her up and sending her off to finishing school.

And her life would be over at sixteen.

So Charlotte smoothed the lace of her dress — an anemic-looking ecru that Lady Diane insisted was the height of fashion — and pasted on her best smile. She pointed herself in the direction of the party and stepped onto the lawn.

As she passed the new footman, Lawrence, Charlotte used her imagination to turn him into a dashing cavalier. Those high cheekbones and extraordinarily dark blue eyes were just too enchanting to be wasted on a mere manservant. He would have to be a deposed Italian prince, who would carry her off to live in a community of poets and adventurers who never talked about the weather.

"Think it will rain?"

Charlotte came crashing back to The Manor and her mother's garden party. Lord Andrew Broadhurst hovered near her right elbow.

Safe, dependable, ever-present Andrew Broadhurst. With his dependably brown hair flopping over one dependably brown eye, dressed dependably in white linen and a straw boater hat.

Eighteen, heir to the Earl of Ashdown, with a good head for business and cricket and not much else. Lady Diane loved him, despite his rather quirky habit of asking how the pudding was made. *Perfect marriage material.*

The sun beat down on the back of Charlotte's neck, making her feel itchy and cross. She opened her mouth to snipe, but over Andrew's shoulder, she saw her mother watching.

So Charlotte lifted her chin a little and tipped her head to one side, smiling up at him from just beneath the veil of her new hat.

"Why, yes," she said. "Yes, I think it will." Adding in her mind, *Eventually*. It always rained in England eventually. It would be September on Friday. Surely the drought couldn't last forever.

Andrew frowned up at the sky — a clear blue like something found in a hand-painted photograph.

Charlotte took the temporary distraction as a gift and used it to excuse herself, earning a glare from her mother but also a chance to breathe again beneath her corset, which seemed to tighten every time Andrew approached.

Skirting the edge of the party, Charlotte sought relief in the shade of the canopy and in the company of Frances Caldwell, her only friend in the entire crowd.

"What have you been daydreaming about?" Fran asked. Her blonde hair was cut daringly short, and perfectly framed her heart-shaped face, the corner of her little bow mouth tipped up into a teasing smile.

"Escape." Charlotte cast a quick look at her mother, hoping she was less observant than Fran.

"And the new footman," Fran whispered. "I can tell."

Then she turned and waved Lawrence over.

Charlotte felt a blush start to rise and tried suppressing it with thoughts of throwing Fran into The Manor's lake. But Fran just swiped a lemon ice from Lawrence's tray and thanked him politely. Lawrence inclined his head and turned away.

"He *is* handsome," Fran said before he walked out of earshot. Charlotte thought she saw Lawrence hesitate as if waiting to hear her reply, his head turned slightly so she could see the line of his jaw.

Charlotte imagined herself coming up with the perfect reply. But she couldn't in real life. She hesitated for so long, Lawrence carried the ices to the rest of the guests and Fran changed the subject.

"Where are your brothers?" Fran asked, craning her neck to look at the guests, and then up at The Manor itself. She innocently studied the Tudor brick façade and the long stripes of windows that reflected the sky. Charlotte heard the feigned indifference in her friend's voice and knew Fran was really asking about Charlotte's eldest brother, David.

"Out," Charlotte said and smiled.

"All *five* of them?" Fran choked.

"London, Army, Navy, Cambridge, boating." Charlotte ticked them off on her fingers. Her brothers weren't imprisoned at The Manor. They could do *anything*.

"No wonder the party is dull." Fran rolled her eyes. "Your mother is a fashionable hostess, but she doesn't invite any eligible *men*."

Charlotte laughed. "There's always *Lord* Andrew Broadhurst."

"He's really quite appealing in the right light," Fran said. They both turned to watch him. He stood at the very edge of the lawn and appeared to be in earnest conversation with

Lawrence while the ices melted. Probably about the weather. Despite Fran's assessment, Charlotte thought the light favored the footman. She sighed.

"He's rich," Fran pronounced. "You could do worse, Charlotte."

"Maybe I want to do better."

"You think you can marry a duke?"

"I want to fall in love."

Fran stuck out her lower lip and blew a curl off her forehead, which Charlotte took as a show of contempt.

Sometimes Fran reminded Charlotte of Lady Diane. Perhaps it was because Fran wanted to marry David and become the next lady of The Manor. And seeing that the current lady was deep in conversation with Fran's mother, it looked like that might be a distinct possibility.

"Who is that?" Fran asked suddenly.

Charlotte craned her neck. All she saw were neighbors. Her mother's friends.

"Who is who?" she asked.

"No, you little owl." Fran laughed and put her face next to Charlotte's. She pointed *past* the party, to where the lawn met the trees. "Her."

The girl definitely wasn't a party guest. Gray cotton dress, thick black stockings, and sensible black shoes. Her brown hair in its bun turned reddish in the sunlight. She glanced back over her shoulder quickly, giving Charlotte a split-second view of her face, then walked away, her stride purposeful.

"The kitchen maid?"

"Is that a question or a statement?" Fran raised an eyebrow. "Is The Manor so big that you don't know your own staff?"

It was, actually. The upstairs alone required twenty servants — from the very visible and utterly formal butler, Foyle, to the hall boy who could only be seen if one woke up early enough to catch him carrying the wood to the fireplaces. There was no telling how many staff worked in the stables, laundry, gardens, scullery, and kitchens. Downstairs was *terra incognita* — an entirely different world, populated by myths and wraiths and an ever-changing array of workers.

But Fran sounded so . . . accusatory.

"It was a statement," Charlotte said emphatically, and seized on the information that appeared in the deep recesses of her mind. "Her name is Jenny. I think she broke her collarbone diving off the ha-ha a couple of years ago."

"How positively irresponsible of her," Fran replied. "Why isn't she in the kitchen?"

Charlotte wasn't sure she cared. "Getting more cress from the garden for the sandwiches?"

Fran turned to face her. "*That* is not where the gardens are. *That* is the way to the rockery and the lake."

Fran stood with her arms akimbo, her gloved fists resting on the minty green skirts of her day dress. Demanding an answer.

Charlotte could only shrug.

"You don't even care that one of your staff members is wandering away in the middle of a party?" Fran asked. "What if she dives off the ha-ha again?"

"Does it matter?" Charlotte's irritation rose with Fran's questioning. "Maybe it's her afternoon off."

"During a *party*?" Fran said. "She should be in the kitchen. That girl is definitely up to something."

Charlotte imagined the kitchen maid meeting a boy in the forest, trading locks of hair and kisses. Or perhaps she was selling secrets to a spy.

Not that The Manor had any secrets to keep.

Fran grabbed Charlotte's hand and started dragging her across the lawn. "We're going to find out."

"We can't just leave." Charlotte tugged her hand out of Fran's grip. She glanced at the empty space next to Lady Diane, still waiting to be filled.

Charlotte imagined walking past it, not caring what was expected of her. She was always brave and spontaneous in her imagination. It was the only way to continue to be herself in real life.

Just once, Charlotte wanted to do the unexpected. Be irresponsible. She watched Jenny's straight back disappear around the corner of The Manor. Fran was right. The kitchen maid couldn't have the afternoon off. *That* was a spontaneous girl.

Charlotte followed Fran around the edge of the party, trying to appear casual. She caught Lawrence watching her, but she quickly looked away and increased her pace until she reached the shelter of the woods.

Walking beneath the canopy of the trees was like walking into a cave. The temperature dropped, the light disappeared. Charlotte had to blink a few times to adjust her eyes, and a prickle of gooseflesh ran up her arms.

Her mother didn't let her go into the woods alone. Lady Diane said mud was for men, and the state of the gun room proved it. But the days without rain had solidified the woodland path and turned the fallen leaves brittle and whispery.

Up ahead, the kitchen maid's dress had disappeared into the gloom, but Fran's pale silk glowed ghostly in the freckled light. Charlotte followed this like a beacon. They wove between the trees and around the artfully tumbled boulders of the rockery and down the slope to the lake.

She caught up to Fran, who was pressed up against the trunk of a wide, ancient oak, peering around it.

The kitchen maid, Jenny (or was it Jean?), paused on the muddy bank, then sat down on a rock and removed her shoes and rolled off her stockings.

"What is she doing?" Fran gasped. "It's indecent!"

Gingerly, the kitchen maid stood and walked to the mud at the edge of the lake, her toes in the water and her face lifted to the sky above. The very picture of bliss.

Not indecent at all.

The water looked so cool. So inviting. So much nicer than the garden party. Charlotte wished she could trade places with the kitchen maid. Wished she had that much freedom. She curled her toes inside her kid leather slippers, imagining they were digging into the mud. Felt the caress of the water as she stepped farther in.

"She shouldn't be doing that," Fran said, her mouth a firm line. "She should be working."

"She's just cooling off," Charlotte started to say, but Fran stepped out from behind the tree and shouted.

"Jenny!" she cried. "I say, Jenny!"

The kitchen maid spun around so fast, she almost slipped.

Fran marched down the slope. The other girl saw her and scrambled to her discarded stockings.

"This is private property," Fran said. "Not yours."

The kitchen maid lifted her chin defiantly. "I live here," she said.

"You *work* here," Fran replied, condescension freezing her tone. She sounded like Lady Diane. "And you'd do well to remember who your betters are. Now, put your shoes on and go back to it. Before you find you have no job to go back to."

The defiance left the other girl's face immediately. She slipped her muddy feet into her shoes, balled her stockings into her fist, and walked past Fran without another word.

Charlotte attempted to hide herself behind the oak tree. To distance herself from Fran's arrogance. But the kitchen maid saw Charlotte's movement and stopped, staring.

Charlotte saw a little of her own fear mirrored in the other girl's hazel eyes.

Charlotte tried to look in charge. Tried to look like she would fire someone on the spot for being disobedient. But she knew she couldn't take the longing out of her eyes. The longing to be able to take off *her* stockings and paddle in the lake.

The kitchen maid dipped her head and walked on.

Fran slapped her hands together. "Job done," she crowed and strode back up to Charlotte. "Back to the party."

"Why don't we do that?" Charlotte asked without thinking.

"What?"

"Take our stockings off. Wade in the lake."

Fran laughed. "You do have a fanciful imagination, Charlotte."

Charlotte hesitated. "It looked . . . nice."

"It's mucky. And full of crawly things."

Charlotte tried to smile. "Now who has the fanciful imagination?"

But something about the look on the kitchen maid's face when she dipped her feet in the water wouldn't leave her be. The possibility of adventure. Of relief. No matter how small.

"I think I'll brave the crawly things," Charlotte said, surprising herself.

Fran narrowed her eyes. "*You* are not a kitchen maid, Charlotte Edmonds."

"You're right," Charlotte said, her conviction growing stronger. "I'm not. I don't have a job I need to do."

"Oh, yes, you do. Your job is to be hostess. To be at your mother's side. You may not be making the finger sandwiches and pots of tea, but you have a job to do, just like she does."

Charlotte hesitated. But only for an instant. Then she turned and walked down to the water.

"I can't lose mine," she called. *Even if I wanted to.* If the kitchen maid was willing to take the risk to cool off in the lake, surely Charlotte could.

She looked back up to where Fran was frowning at her.

"I won't cover for you," Fran said.

Charlotte felt a rush of exhilaration. "I don't need you to."

Fran blew the hair off her face, turned on her heel, and stomped back along the path.

Only then did Charlotte begin to question herself.

She turned back to the lake. On the far shore, duckweed lapped against the rocks, but otherwise the water was clear, reflecting the silhouettes of trees against the sky. She sat on a boulder and removed her shoes and stockings. Then she looked over her shoulder at the shadows and the trees, Fran's condemnation ringing in her memory. *Indecent.*

But if Charlotte could not see the lawn and the party guests, they couldn't see her.

Charlotte grinned wickedly, lifted her skirts, and walked to the verge of the lake. She was a lady adventuress, on a distant beach, about to dip her toes into the Pacific Ocean. She closed her eyes and wiggled her toes, feeling the mud ooze between them. She lifted her face to the sky, imitating the kitchen maid, and felt the tension ease from the back of her neck.

And something crawling up the back of her leg.

Charlotte jumped and kicked spasmodically. There was a splash as *whatever-it-was* hit the lake. Charlotte looked for it, but saw nothing but the rippling sky. She turned to see if anything else might be creeping up on her and saw nothing but her own footprints.

And the hem of her dress dragging through them. The silk streaked where the water soaked up into the fabric. The eyelets of the lace plugged with mud.

Lady Diane would disown her.

"Oh, no," she moaned. There was no way she could hide it. No way she could go back to the party.

And nowhere else she could go.

She wished for rescue. For the dashing cavalier.

"Lady Charlotte!" a male voice called out.

Charlotte didn't know if she should call out in return or run. Maybe she could hide herself in the lake.

"I'm here?" she finally called, hating that her voice made it more of a question than an answer.

"Lady Charlotte." Lawrence the footman appeared from the gloom. "Your mother is concerned about your absence." He stopped, his eyes on her bare feet.

*Indecent.*

"I can't go back like this," Charlotte said, squeezing her eyes shut, as if that would prevent him from seeing her.

"True," Lawrence said. "And we can't let you in through the front of the house like that, either. Mr. Foyle would have a fit."

Charlotte's eyes flew open. He was looking at her as if she were a puzzle to be solved. Not a flagrant delinquent who deserved the wrath she was sure to incur. He caught her staring at him, and he winked.

"Servants' entrance," he said confidently. "The only thing for it."

Charlotte took a step toward him. And another. Then stopped. Afraid.

"My shoes," she said to cover up, and looked down at the pristine eggshell silk of her slippers. She would ruin them. She went through all the things she'd already done that day that her mother would punish her for. Leaving the party. Going into the lake. Muddying her dress.

Being alone in the woods with the footman.

"In for a penny, in for a pound, I suppose," she said with forced gaiety and stepped into her shoes, cringing at the slick wetness.

"We'll get you inside safely," Lawrence said with a gallant bow.

Definitely dashing.

Charlotte followed him through the woods. They kept

the little hill and the rotunda between themselves and the garden party in order to approach The Manor from the east. The house seemed to rise from the earth of its own volition. The cupola over the marble hall was just visible over the roof line.

Lawrence motioned for her to stop, then crept forward behind a giant beech. Charlotte held her breath while he peered around the tree and then returned to her.

"The party is on the other side of the patio," he whispered into her ear, his breath tickling her hair a little. Charlotte breathed in the scents of soap and lemon, almost forgetting her predicament. "The wall should hide us. If we run low, we can avoid being seen."

She followed him across the lawn, her heart beating tight against her corset. She didn't look left or right, but kept her eyes on Lawrence's back the entire time. Together, they went through the kitchen courtyard and down the basement steps.

It truly was another world. The brick-floored hall illuminated only by the stepping-stones of light coming from the doorways along it. And the sounds of clanging pots and barked orders riding the waves of heat emanating from the kitchen.

No wonder the kitchen maid had escaped to the lake.

Charlotte hadn't been downstairs since she was five. Back when her brothers thought it would be fun to sneak a cute little girl into the servants' hall to cover stealing cakes from the kitchen and flirting with the housemaids.

Lady Diane had forbidden any excursions to the basement after she found Charlotte playing pat-a-cake with the biscuit dough and David in a clinch with the second housemaid. David was sent back to Oxford, and the girl was sent packing without a reference.

Charlotte stopped.

"I shouldn't be here," she whispered, and then realized with horror that she spoke the truth. She looked up at Lawrence. His dark hair fell casually over his forehead. And those eyes.

"I promised to get you to safety." Lawrence's tone brooked no disagreement.

But then the kitchen maid swung around the corner and froze, staring at the two of them so close together. Then she looked down at the mud caking the hem of Charlotte's dress.

From the depths of the kitchen, a voice Charlotte recognized as the cook's called out, making the kitchen maid jump.

"The *parsley*, Janie Mae! Her Ladyship is on the warpath!"

Charlotte frowned. Had the cook called the kitchen maid *Janie*?

"Yes, Ma!" the kitchen maid called, without looking away from Charlotte. The recesses of Charlotte's brain dug up another fact — this girl was the cook's daughter. And she was probably about Charlotte's age.

The kitchen maid — Janie — took two steps forward and lowered her voice. "Can I help you, Lady Charlotte?"

"I'm taking her up the servants' stairs," Lawrence said.

"No, you're not, Lawrence," the girl hissed. "If anyone catches the two of you alone together, you'll be out on the street before you can say Jack Robinson."

Lawrence took a step back, looking less like a cavalier and more like a boy afraid of a caning.

"But he's helping me," Charlotte argued. "We're not doing anything wrong."

Janie raised an eyebrow. "Begging your pardon, Lady Charlotte, but gossip spreads faster than fire. And some people only say what they see, not the way things really are."

It sounded worse than the London tearooms. Charlotte felt even more out of place in this downstairs world than she had moments before.

"I'll go through the front entrance," Charlotte said, trying to sound brave. It was, after all, where she belonged.

One of the bells on the wall twitched and rang with a deep, throaty boom. Lawrence and Janie both froze. An instant later the bell rang again.

Something crashed in the kitchen. "Where is that bloody footman?" the cook bellowed.

Janie grabbed Lawrence by the shoulders and spun him around, pushing him down the long hall. "Go."

Lawrence didn't look back.

Janie turned to Charlotte, wide-eyed. "That was the bell for the marble hall."

"How do you know?"

"The ring. Every bell has a certain ring."

"There's someone up there?" Charlotte asked.

"Your mother is up there." Janie bit her lip. "She's the only one who rings twice."

Charlotte felt light-headed. Spots appeared in the corners of her vision and she looked down at her filthy skirts. Why did her mother demand she wear ecru? And why did Charlotte think she could have an adventure?

"You went into the lake?"

Charlotte looked up again to see the kitchen maid studying her.

"It just looked too inviting," Charlotte said. She wiggled her toes, still sticky with mud inside her slippers.

"I know."

They stood, staring at each other for just a moment. Understanding.

"I'll take you upstairs."

Janie slipped by her, and Charlotte followed her down the corridor, the bricks uneven beneath her feet. She followed the kitchen maid past the open door of a long, empty room, dominated by a single table and multiple chairs, an upright piano at the far end. Then past a little sitting room.

"Up here." Janie led her up a flight of stairs cut short by a sharp corner. When Charlotte rounded it, she saw that the stairs continued upward, bend after bend. To her left was a plain door covered in green baize like a billiard table. But Janie continued up, her feet silent on the bare wood. At each landing was another green baize door.

Charlotte had lived in The Manor all her life, but she had never felt so turned around. There were no windows in the stairwell. The only light was provided by the oil lamp Janie had brought along.

The stairs went up into the darkness until Charlotte thought surely they must be at the roof. She struggled to breathe against her corset and paused on a narrow landing. A shard of brilliant light appeared as Janie pushed open a door and peered through the crack.

"All clear."

On the other side of the door, stark and wintry electric light gleamed on the white walls and elaborately framed paintings. This was the second-story hallway. Charlotte paused, getting her bearings. Her room was two doors down, on the left. She stepped out onto the thick hall carpet.

She turned back to see Janie still on the landing, the fingers of one hand wrapped around the door.

"Can you come to my room?" Charlotte asked. "I . . ." What did she want? For the adventure to continue? She didn't want to admit that she could barely dress herself. And looking at this girl, who could make food and find solutions and go down to the lake on her own, Charlotte felt ashamed that she was so helpless.

"I can't." Janie looked right at her and shook her head. "I don't belong upstairs."

"All right," Charlotte said. She turned away. But she found that she didn't want to go. Didn't want to go back to her room, change her dress, face her mother. Didn't want to leave the warm yellow glow of the dimly lit servants' stairs.

She turned to thank Janie for her kindness. But the door had already closed, only a slim straight line betraying its existence.

# CHAPTER 2

On her five a.m. trek down the servants' stairs from her attic room, Janie Seward paused on the second-floor landing. Her fingers itched to open the door. To see once again the thick carpet, the paintings in their gilt frames. To catch the scents of luxury.

She placed her hand on the door and listened. The entire Manor was asleep. She could just . . . look. No one would ever know.

For a moment, she fought helplessly against the invisible barrier. The one that kept the servants in their places. The one that should have kept Lady Charlotte Edmonds out of the kitchen yesterday.

"I know where I belong," Janie murmured. She hoisted her candle aloft and continued down the stairs to the kitchen.

It was still sweltering. Janie quickly passed it by and opened the scullery door to the courtyard. The relief was immediate, the early morning air flowing like mercury down the basement stairs — thick, cool, and silvery with the dawn.

Janie glanced once at the empty kitchen, then ran up the stairs and through the courtyard. She stopped at the gate, looking out over the hills of the Weald and the mist still clinging to the ash trees down by the River Eden.

Eden.

Janie sucked in a deep breath, closed her eyes, and lifted her face to the sky. She loved The Manor in the morning, before anyone else was awake. She loved to breathe in the smells of sweet grass and chestnut trees in summer, the frost and wood smoke in winter.

Janie remembered the words of Miss Caldwell yesterday. "You *work* here," she had said. But Janie felt she lived here more than the family who owned it. They missed so much, all tied up in their clothes and jewels and newspapers. They had those big, wide windows in every room and never looked out of them.

The morning star shimmered in the haze and Janie breathed out, wishing on it. Then she turned and reentered the kitchen. It was probably her last breath of fresh air for the day.

Yesterday, her spontaneous decision to play truant down at the lake during the garden party had very nearly been a disaster. It still could be, if little Miss Charlotte decided to tell Lady Diane. Janie's pay could be docked. Or worse. She knew better than to do anything that might jeopardize her position.

It wouldn't happen again.

Mollie was not in the scullery yet. She was supposed to light the donkey boiler so the house could have hot water, but Janie did it for her.

"That's not your job, you know."

Janie turned to see Harry Peasgood, the hall boy, leaning against the door frame, grinning at her.

"I know," she said, standing and brushing her dirty hands on her apron. The hierarchy among the servants was as strict as it was among the aristocracy. Everyone knew his or her place, and everyone held on as tightly as they could, never deigning to stoop a little bit lower, even to help the less fortunate.

"No one ever did it for you when you were a skivvy," Harry added. Janie heard the bitterness in his voice. Harry had been hall boy since he was twelve. At seventeen, he should be moving up to footman. But Lady Diane thought he wasn't handsome enough. She liked her footmen tall and dark and effortlessly dashing. Harry had yet to reach her six-foot standard, and his sand-colored curls were cropped close, squashed by sleep on one side.

"*You* did, Harry," Janie said and rubbed his head, making the curls stand up again. "That's why I do it for Mollie. The poor girl was crying again yesterday."

Harry ducked out of reach. "Tea?" he asked, and started to fill the kettle before she could reply. "You're a bit late this morning."

"Had to visit the view," Janie explained, and went to the pantry. She measured flour into a bowl and cradled it in the crook of her right arm, then hefted the sugar, baking powder, and salt with her left, carrying them back to the scarred oak table.

Every morning was the same, ever since her first day as scullery maid four years before, when Harry found her cursing at the donkey boiler. He had cleared the coal dust, lit the fire, and made her a cup of tea. After that, they always spent the pre-waking hours at The Manor as a team. She would clean the range while he stoked the fire, knead the bread while he brought in more coal. Together, they shared the first scones off the pan.

And the quiet before the storm.

Janie watched Harry as he checked the flue of the second stove. His back had grown broader, his hands more capable. His face had lost most of its boyishness, but he was still Harry.

"Has this been drawing properly?" He turned and caught her staring.

Janie quickly looked down at the dough she was kneading. "We've been trying not to use it because of the heat."

"You'll have to for the shooting party. Double the guests. I'll take a look at it later today."

"This house wouldn't run without you, Harry Peasgood."

Harry hefted a bucket of water onto the table. "I have no illusions of my importance here, Janie. Look at this." He stuck his hand into the water and then looked up at her. "See my hand?"

"Of course I do. It's in my clean water."

Harry didn't laugh. He watched her as he drew his hand out of the bucket, making sure she saw what he was doing. "See that water? Think it notices my absence? Well, neither will anyone here."

It was true the downstairs staff at The Manor changed regularly. Laundresses, kitchen maids, gardeners' boys. They were invisible. Didn't even have names — if Lady Charlotte wanted to call Janie *Jenny*, she'd be Jenny.

But Harry had been there for years. He'd opened the tradesman's door to her when she'd arrived — half-starved and silent — returning to a birthplace she'd never seen and a mother she didn't know. He was one of the reasons The Manor felt like home.

"I would notice," Janie blurted.

Harry grinned. "Only because I wouldn't be around to make your tea in the morning." He poured the water away and refilled the bucket, putting it back on the table so she could use it to clean up.

Janie's throat tightened, but she didn't say anything. She put the scones in the oven and sliced the bread while Harry poured the just-boiled water over the tea leaves. She slathered a thick slice with butter and strawberry jam, and traded it for the mug of milky tea he held out to her.

His eyes were such a beguiling color, like tea. Brown and gold — warm and comforting.

"Eat that," she said, putting as much of a tease into her voice as she could muster. "And get to work."

"I will when I finish doing yours." Harry laughed and danced away before Janie could land the punch she aimed at his arm.

Janie scraped the leftover knots of dough into the pig bucket. "I guess breakfast won't make itself."

"You really should get Mollie down here earlier. She's supposed to wake *you* up. And you can't do two jobs at once."

"I've been doing it for this long — why stop now?" Janie said, going to the larder for the bacon. Even when she was in the scullery, she had taken on extra cooking jobs just to learn. Anything the kitchen maids didn't want to do, Janie did.

But that wasn't the real reason. The reason she couldn't say out loud except in a tease.

"Besides," she said, returning to the table, "maybe I just want you all to myself."

Harry choked on his bread and chased it with a gulp of tea.

"I guess I just don't like change," Janie amended, focusing on slicing the bacon into thin strips. "I like things the way they are."

She loved the quiet of the early mornings before the kitchen whirled into well-controlled chaos. She liked having a friend.

"Change is inevitable, Janie," Harry said, finishing off the bread. "You don't want to be a skivvy all your life."

Janie slammed her knife down on the table. "I am *not* a skivvy," she said heatedly. "I am a kitchen maid."

Harry held very still, watching her. "Do you really want to spend your life in service? I can't believe you want to be a kitchen maid forever."

No, she didn't. But she didn't want Harry Peasgood telling her so.

"My mother is in service," she said, picking up the knife again and laying each slice of bacon on the broiler tray. "My grandparents were in service. My great-grandparents. My father tried to better himself. He joined the Army. And died in South Africa before I even knew what he looked like. I make a good kitchen maid. I do my job and keep my place. My entire life is mapped out for me."

"There are no maps of life, Janie," Harry said. "My parents were in service, too. But what if I want something different? What if I want to go to uni and become an engineer?"

"You watch what you say, Harry Peasgood; Lady Diane would tell you that you're trying to get above yourself. *Be content with your station in life.*" Janie did a good imitation of Her Ladyship's clipped articulation and pinched way of looking over her nose at people. It was exactly what Lady Diane had said and exactly the way she had said it when Mrs. Seward asked if Janie could attend the local secondary school.

"Maybe I don't want my station in life," Harry said. "I have options. I could work in a factory or move to America where there isn't all this hierarchy and status. Workers are fighting to be paid fairly — look at the dockworkers' strikes. Things are changing. We have more choices than ever."

Janie tried to look into the grand future Harry thought he was describing. But she couldn't picture the servants being equal. Couldn't picture a house with no servants at all, unless it was one where poverty crushed the occupants and slid them toward starvation — like the years she'd spent with her aunt and uncle on Romney Marsh. The men who spent their days bent over a plow, the boys who spent weeks at a time following the sheep whose wool would sell for a few pennies.

The family that ate for an entire week off the amount of bacon she would put on the servants' table for just one morning.

"Maybe I don't want choices," she said. "Maybe I want to be a cook. Here. At The Manor."

"Your mother is The Manor's cook," Harry said mildly. "You'll have to leave eventually."

"I'm not leaving!"

Janie's shout rang down the hall like the bells that called the servants. Harry froze but Janie kept moving. She threw the tray of bacon in the oven, lifted her hands, and pushed him.

"After spending years on the Marsh with barely enough to eat. After the death of my father and the final return of my mother, I am back in the place I was born, Harry. I belong here."

Janie's voice cracked and she slumped a little, blinking hard not to shed the tears, trying to regain some of her anger so she could shout instead of cry.

Harry reached for her, but Janie twitched her shoulder out from under his hand. She looked up at him, her eyes dry.

"I'm not leaving," she said again.

"Who's leaving?" Mollie the scullery maid walked in, her blonde hair in a messy knot.

"No one," Janie said, looking at Harry pointedly.

"I wouldn't dare," Harry said. "And there's always wood to chop and shoes to polish, so I guess for now, I'm indispensable." He swiped a freshly baked scone off the tray and winked at Janie before leaving the kitchen.

But the wink didn't cover up the hurt in his eyes.

"I wish I could leave," Mollie said, her voice small and sad. Her hands were already red and raw and she hadn't even started washing dishes yet.

Janie sighed. She felt guilty enough for shouting at Harry; she couldn't scold Mollie for coming down late. "Sit down a minute."

"I can't," the other girl said. "I haven't even lit the boiler." Tears sprang up, and Janie envied the ease with which Mollie shed them.

"It's done," Janie said briskly. "Now sit and hold out your hands."

Janie rubbed Mollie's hands in honey and then wrapped them in oatmeal and a kitchen cloth. "That will help. Do it again tonight when you're done."

"It won't help."

"It *does*. You forget I was scullery maid for four years." She put her hand under the other girl's chin. "It gets better." *And it gets worse.*

Tess, the head kitchen maid, stepped into the kitchen and stopped short. Glaring.

"You . . ." She pointed at Mollie. ". . . shouldn't be sitting down."

Mollie hopped up and tore off the cloth covering her hands, pushing it at Janie as if trying to shed culpability.

"You should know better." Tess turned to Janie. "We have the shooting party this week. His Lordship arrives tonight and Lord David tomorrow. The Caldwell girl and Lord Broadhurst will be arriving Wednesday, and the rest the day after. The house will be full."

Janie rolled her eyes. She'd been in The Manor kitchen longer than Tess.

Tess gripped her by the shoulders. "Don't think that because you're the cook's daughter, you can get away with skiving off. I'll tell Mrs. Griffiths you've been sitting down when you're supposed to be working."

Janie didn't say that, technically, she hadn't been the one sitting down. She didn't say that Mrs. Griffiths, the housekeeper, wasn't in charge of kitchen staff. She didn't say that she had seen Tess sitting in the servants' hall reading a penny romance the day before when she should have been making the aspic for dinner.

"Don't worry, Tess," Janie said instead. "I know my place. And I always get my work done."

Mollie pushed past her on the way to the scullery as the servants began bustling in, demanding tea and breakfast. The door to the servants' hall was crowded one instant and empty the next as the maids grabbed a scone and bread, and then rushed to clean the lower rooms of the house. As a lowly second kitchen maid, it was Janie's job to cook for and serve them — plain scones, bread, porridge, and bacon — while her mother cooked the sausages, eggs, kidneys, and whatever else the Edmonds family might want for breakfast.

Janie cleared plates with one hand while setting down a fresh batch of scones with the other.

"Fifty-five days without rain," Lawrence said, not looking up from the newspaper spread in front of him. "No wonder it's so bloomin' 'ot."

The butler, Mr. Foyle, strode through the door, prompting all the servants to stand.

"Watch your language and your patois, Lawrence," he said, pulling in his chair as he sat down. "Her Ladyship doesn't appreciate dropped aitches."

Janie caught Lawrence's eye and recognized the thoughts behind them because she was thinking the same thing. Her Ladyship didn't appreciate much at all, and dropped aitches seemed the least of them. Lawrence grinned at her and raised an eyebrow, and she suppressed a smile, knowing Her Ladyship also didn't appreciate flirting between the servants.

"Why don't you sit down, Janie?" Lawrence asked, reaching for the teapot and earning Janie a glare from Sarah, the head housemaid.

"I don't have time to sit down with the likes of you," Janie quipped and returned to the kitchen. Truth be told, after her first cup of tea and slice of bread with Harry, she didn't have time to eat at all. Certainly not sitting down.

A bell rang in the corridor, and the noise from the servants' hall stopped.

"Was that the front entrance bell?" Mollie asked.

Janie nodded, watching Mr. Foyle rush down the passageway, pulling at his cuffs, brushing his waistcoat, and muttering under his breath.

"Who on earth would be arriving at this hour?" Janie heard him say.

"Don't stand there gawping, Janie," Mrs. Seward said, stirring the three pans simmering on the stove and returning to her end of the kitchen table. She waved her little knife. "Get to work! The kedgeree needs to go up hot."

Janie struggled to hide her frown, but not hard enough.

"None of that, my girl," her mother said.

Janie made a face at the starched cap on the top of her mother's head. Kedgeree, with its rice and eggs and smoked fish, seemed a disgusting thing to eat for breakfast, but the lord asked for it every Monday. Something about his time in India.

Her Ladyship hated it. She insisted that the baize on the doors didn't block the reek of the fish from penetrating every floor of the house. But it was one of the few things His Lordship didn't defer to her on. He requested it be served even when he was staying at his London club.

Lady Diane got what she wanted the rest of the time.

"Who do you think is at the door?" Janie asked her mother.

"Not the gardener nor the grocer nor any other delivery, my dear," Mrs. Seward replied. "So it's unlikely to alter our lives in any way."

Mrs. Seward peered into the pot where Janie mixed the rice with the tomatoes and flaked fish.

"Unless they eat kedgeree," the cook murmured. "No one else will, with His Lordship away. I will never in my life understand the rich." She turned back to the kidneys and flipped them with a single movement.

Mr. Foyle reappeared at the kitchen door.

"One more for breakfast," he said. "I hope it's not an inconvenience. Her Ladyship's sister has arrived unexpectedly."

Mrs. Seward didn't turn around, but Janie saw the back of her neck turn pink at the same time the skin of her cheeks turned pale.

"Not an inconvenience, Mr. Foyle." Mrs. Seward's voice was barely audible above the hissing of the kettle.

The kitchen was silent for a moment after the butler left.

"Her Ladyship has a sister?" Janie finally asked.

"Fifteen years younger."

"You know her?"

"I *knew* her," Janie's mother answered after a moment. "And I was wrong before. She could alter our lives just by being here."

# Chapter 3

Charlotte lay in the middle of her bed, her chestnut-brown hair fanning out across her pillows, her hands palm up on the coverlet. She was trying to mimic Ophelia in the Millais painting, but knew she was getting the tragic expression completely wrong.

The head housemaid, Sarah, had already been up to help her dress, but Charlotte had taken her hair out of its plait to practice the pose. Trying to get the feeling right. Summoning the memory of the cool water of the lake the day before.

But all she could remember was the arch of Lawrence's smile when he winked at her.

Charlotte rolled over to the end of her bed and lay on her stomach to open the cedar chest on the floor. She had to stretch as far as she could to get to the bottom of it. She reached past last year's outgrown clothes, shuddering at the touch of the white sateen gown her mother had made her wear to the Coronation in June.

Andrew Broadhurst had stood beside her as they watched the procession of all of Europe's nobility go before them.

And he had yawned.

With a final dive, Charlotte touched the thing she was looking for. A small wooden box, the inlaid top starting to crack a little. That was the reason her mother had decided to get rid of it.

"It's ugly," Lady Diane had said.

But Charlotte loved it. The intricate inlay depicted a scene from China. Women gathered around a river, their clothes like long, satin robes, cinched at the waist. Their hair pulled up into implausibly full buns and pierced with sticks like pincushions. Charlotte's hair would never hold a shape like that. Poker-straight and thick as November rainfall, it barely held its place in a chignon.

Charlotte dug the box out and lifted it onto the bed, opening it carefully. She breathed in the dry scent of paper and the ferrous tang of ink. She slipped off the bed and sat on the floor with the sheaves of paper and the inkpot, keeping the bed and its velvet curtains between herself and the door.

She curled over the pages, reading the words already written. Mostly descriptions of the people around her. Her silent father, her much-older brothers and each of their fetishes — boating or billiards or, in the case of David, girls. She had dozens of pages about the disapproval of her mother. How Charlotte knew she'd never live up to her mother's expectations. How much she wanted to escape.

And then there were her stories. The adventures she imagined, but never got to experience. Sailing to distant lands and traveling by elephant and falling in love.

Pretending to be Ophelia this morning had given her an idea for a story about a girl who fakes her own death in order to run off with a raffish Italian count.

Charlotte smiled as the words spilled out of her imagination, barely giving her time to re-ink her pen. The description of the count was delicious fun. Tall, dark, dashing. With sapphire eyes and a teasing smile.

A quick knock at her door startled her so much she almost knocked over her inkpot. Charlotte blew on the paper to dry her writing and scrambled to put it all back in the little box, the nib of the pen smearing across several of the pages.

The knock came again. More urgently.

Charlotte slammed the lid of the box closed and stood.

Then she threw open the cedar chest and dug the old clothes out of it, shouting, "Come in!" at the same time.

Sarah stopped short at the sight of the gowns and gloves on the floor, and Charlotte thought she saw a flash of disbelief, followed by frustration. But these expressions then disappeared into a blank mask.

"Her Ladyship asked that you come downstairs, Lady Charlotte," Sarah said with a brief curtsey.

"But . . . it's not breakfast time yet." Charlotte stood with her back to the cedar chest, hoping that she had dug the Chinese box deep enough. Hoping that Sarah wouldn't find it. She knew her mother occasionally left coins in odd places to test the maids' integrity — if the coins disappeared, a maid could be fired on the spot. But that didn't mean Sarah wouldn't read her writing if given the opportunity.

"And Mother doesn't go down for breakfast," Charlotte added helplessly.

Sarah moved swiftly through the room, picking things up and laying them across the bed to fold them later. She seemed nervous. Skittish.

"There's a visitor."

"Visitor?" Charlotte allowed herself one quick glance at the chest. She couldn't see the box at all. It was covered by her embroidery. Hidden. "At eight o'clock in the morning?"

"Most unusual, I know," Sarah said.

Charlotte could imagine the same tone amplified in her mother's voice. Disapproving. Judgmental.

Sarah guided Charlotte over to the dressing table and ran a brush through Charlotte's hair, snagging the ends and sending hair flying in the static before taming it into a hastily pinned knot.

"Whoever could it be?" Charlotte mused. The local constabulary come to investigate a murder? A dashing Italian count?

"Your aunt," Sarah said. "Lady Beatrice Smythe."

A long-lost relative.

Her father had no sisters and Lady Diane rarely spoke of hers, who had shocked the family by running off with a rich commoner. Charlotte knew Lady Beatrice had lived at The Manor until she married Mr. Smythe, and then on his plantations in India and Malaya. When he died of yellow fever, she moved to Italy.

As far as Charlotte knew, Lady Beatrice hadn't set foot in England in sixteen years. It seemed strange she would return so suddenly, and without warning.

Charlotte tried to imagine having the courage and the means to make a life for herself somewhere else. But the reality seemed more fanciful than anything she could make up.

Charlotte smoothed the skirt of her pale pink linen visiting dress, suddenly nervous. It was better than the ecru she'd worn yesterday, but the pleated chiffon bodice made her feel horribly provincial. Her aunt would be cosmopolitan. Glamorous. Worldly.

*No wonder Aunt Beatrice never wanted to come back to The Manor,* Charlotte thought as she opened her door.

Charlotte's room was near the end of a long hall, and she had to pass the more elegant and impactful rooms her mother reserved for guests before she could get downstairs. It had always made her feel as if her mother wanted her out of the way.

The grand staircase, with its highly polished solid oak handrails and banks of windows, swept down to the marble hall. The stone floor was inlaid like a chessboard in black and white. Charlotte was surprised to find the hall empty. The very silence seemed to echo.

Then the servants' door behind the staircase opened, and Lawrence stepped through, carrying a tray laden with silver-domed dishes. He looked flustered, and Charlotte clearly heard Mrs. Seward's voice call, "Come back for the kidneys!" Lawrence nodded once, though there was no way Mrs. Seward could see him, then he looked up and saw Charlotte, motionless in the center of the hall, both feet on the same black marble square.

Charlotte smiled. She meant it to be casual — a mistress politely acknowledging a servant. But she felt it stretch across her face. It even made her shoulders relax and her ribs crush against her corset.

Lawrence smiled back — a quick dimple and a light in his eyes. But he erased the smile immediately and replaced it with a mask of professional detachment.

"Lady Charlotte," he said, his voice like a caress in the quiet of the hall. "The rest of the . . . family is in the dining room."

As Charlotte preceded him across the hall, she wondered if she felt his eyes on her. Wondered if her hair had stayed in place, if he could see the curve of the back of her neck. Then she heard her mother's voice, even through the thick oak of the door.

"But why are you *here*?"

Charlotte hesitated. Lady Diane hated family "nonsense," as she called it. She must be unnerved by Aunt Beatrice's arrival to be so vociferous. And so loud.

Charlotte glanced back at Lawrence, but his face remained impassive. Lady Diane hated even more for servants to know her business. She was always convinced they were gossiping about her.

But Charlotte knew Lawrence wouldn't tell any secrets. He would understand. He would protect her, just as he had at the lake.

Charlotte couldn't hear the reply, but heard the voice. Softer. Quieter. Like a remembered melody. She suddenly wanted to stand in the hall with her ear pressed against the door. To hear what her mother and aunt would say to each other in private — or what they thought was private. But Lawrence waited behind her with his tray, so she stepped forward and entered the dining room.

The morning light spilled across the hills in the distance and angled through the glass of the north-facing windows. Her mother stood, almost silhouetted against the green, her back more rigid than normal, her mouth turned down in a shadowed scowl.

"Charlotte," she said briskly, and then waited while Lawrence laid out the dishes on the sideboard.

Charlotte looked to the opposite end of the room, where a huge framed painting of a seventeenth-century ancestor dominated the wall and dwarfed the woman standing beneath it. Aunt Beatrice didn't look like the younger version of Lady Diane that Charlotte had expected. She had the same fine features, the same slender nose, but her hair was more honey than blonde and her hazel eyes held more warmth than Lady

Diane's steely blue ones. And Aunt Beatrice's mouth turned up into a smile. She wore a traveling dress in a fetching chartreuse that Lady Diane would surely classify as "vulgar" and didn't appear to be wearing a corset — her posture was far too relaxed.

Charlotte heard the door click closed as Lawrence left the room.

"This is your aunt Beatrice," Lady Diane said. "Beatrice, this is Charlotte."

Aunt Beatrice stepped forward, her arms beginning to lift as if she would hug Charlotte or perhaps kiss her on both cheeks like the French. Something Continental and artistic and foreign.

But Lady Diane moved first. "My youngest," she told Beatrice, stepping between them. "My daughter." Charlotte felt a flicker of surprise that her mother would bother to introduce her at all.

Lady Diane pointed to the pot and cups already laid on the table. "Tea."

Charlotte heard the command in her mother's voice.

"I prefer coffee in the morning," Aunt Beatrice said, and didn't move.

Charlotte gaped. It was the first time in her life she had seen someone disregard one of her mother's orders.

Aunt Beatrice met her eye and smiled. "I've learned quite a bit in Italy."

Charlotte wasn't sure if she meant drinking coffee or her open defiance of Lady Diane. Aunt Beatrice looked so small, slight, *young*. But she didn't have to listen to Lady Diane. Aunt Beatrice was a woman in her own right. She'd traveled the world with her husband. She'd lived alone in Italy for over a decade. She was independent.

Lady Diane sat at the table and stared at them both. Pointedly.

Obediently, Charlotte sat. Had some tea. She knew better than to ask the hundreds of questions that hurtled through her imagination and prickled the back of her throat. So she listened to the silence that reverberated between the two women until it roared in her ears, punctuated by the clinking of silverware and the gentle chime of cups and saucers.

She noticed that Aunt Beatrice ate the kedgeree. No one but Charlotte's father ever ate kedgeree. Lady Diane hated it — the sight and the smell. Charlotte imagined herself sitting on a palm-shaded patio overlooking a tea plantation in India, eating kedgeree and listening to the distant call of elephants.

Aunt Beatrice smiled at her.

Lady Diane glared.

Charlotte gazed at the leaves at the bottom of her cup, wondering if they mapped out her future — her presentation at court next year followed by the Season with its balls and dinners and soirees? Or perhaps the dreaded finishing school first. Marriage and children? Or maybe something more adventurous. She wondered if coffee, once consumed, provided the same kind of insight.

"Charlotte." Lady Diane's voice interrupted her reverie. "A word."

Her mother stood, and etiquette demanded that Charlotte and her aunt rise with her.

Lady Diane started for the door, and Aunt Beatrice moved to follow her. Lady Diane turned swiftly.

"Beatrice," she said, "you may tour the house and grounds if you like. You'll find that nothing much has changed."

"I can see that you might think that," Aunt Beatrice replied.

Lady Diane didn't respond. She left the room without a word or backward glance, expecting Charlotte to follow without question or dawdling. But Charlotte did pause in the doorway, and looked back once at her aunt.

Beatrice cocked her head to one side and smiled wryly. "Some things never change."

Flustered, Charlotte followed her mother across the marble checkerboard to the sitting room that looked out over the circular drive and the ornamental garden beyond. Her mother liked to keep an eye on the comings and goings in the house. But Aunt Beatrice's early and sudden arrival had taken even her by surprise. Charlotte noticed that her mother's hair wasn't entirely coiffed in the back — a shamble of curls escaped the pins as if she had pulled away from her maid in a rush to greet her sister.

"Your aunt is here for a visit," Lady Diane said as soon as Charlotte had closed the door of the sitting room. "This puts us in a very awkward position with the shooting party."

Charlotte nodded slowly. One extra person shouldn't make that much difference, considering they would soon be inundated with guests.

"She's welcome here, of course," Lady Diane said. "But . . ."

Lady Diane paused. That one word contradicted the entire sentence before it. And Charlotte wondered what her aunt could possibly have done to make her so *un*welcome at The Manor.

"But I don't want you spending too much time with her," Lady Diane finished. "You need to pay attention to our other guests. Especially Lord Andrew Broadhurst."

Only years of training and practice kept Charlotte from rolling her eyes. But her mother leapt onto her hesitation like a cat on a mouse.

"*Especially* Lord Broadhurst," Lady Diane repeated. She looked Charlotte up and down as one might a new servant. Or a horse. Critically, and with instant appraisal and judgment. Charlotte suddenly worried that her own hair had been too hastily done. She fought the urge to touch it.

"He's the heir to the earldom," Lady Diane said quietly, almost to herself.

And being the oldest son of the Earl of Ashdown made Andrew Broadhurst endlessly attractive.

To Lady Diane.

Charlotte worked up her courage to disagree with her mother. Dispute her. Deflect her as Aunt Beatrice had.

"I'd like to get to know my aunt," Charlotte said lamely.

"There's nothing to know. She's my younger sister. She has no children. And she's leaving. Soon."

Obviously, Lady Diane thought that was the whole story. Everything Charlotte needed to know. Her tone brooked no argument and no questions. But Charlotte's imagination was already inventing a long and tragic history for Aunt Beatrice. Love and loss, travel and adventure. Charlotte turned Aunt

Beatrice into a lady explorer, discoverer of unseen lands and uncharted heartbreak. Returned to the family to . . .

What?

"You'd be wise not to listen to a word she says." Lady Diane's almost offhand remark interrupted Charlotte's reverie.

Charlotte studied her mother. It was the *almost* offhandedness that alarmed her. Lady Diane was never nonchalant. She never said anything without weighing all the consequences first. The tone was too casual to be casual.

"Yes, Mother," Charlotte said finally.

But she couldn't just pretend her aunt didn't exist. And even she couldn't imagine what had caused the estrangement between the two sisters. In her mind, it became a mystery of Sherlock Holmesian proportions.

So she decided to discover what brought her aunt to The Manor. And what caused her mother to wish she were gone.

Every detective needed a sidekick. Someone clever and scrupulous with an innate everyday knowledge. A Watson.

And Charlotte knew just where to find her.

# Chapter 4

Janie flopped into a chair in the servants' hall just after three, and dropped her head onto her forearms on the table. Sarah, the head housemaid, tutted down at the other end. But she'd been sitting for an hour, sewing new lace onto the hem of Lady Charlotte's ecru day dress to cover the stain left by the mud.

Janie had just finished making the next day's bread, scrubbing the kitchen table, and washing the three copper saucepans Mollie had "forgotten" under the scullery sink.

"No rest for the wicked," Lawrence said, resting his palms on the table next to her.

"Then Lady Diane must be a saint," Janie mumbled into the tabletop. "And Lady Charlotte an angel." Guilt immediately followed the words. She had always thought of Charlotte as a small replica of Lady Diane. The nose and voice and demeanor made them appear identical, despite the fact that Lady Charlotte had brown hair and hazel eyes. Kinder eyes. Less judgmental. And that mud on her hem showed clearly that she wasn't as straitlaced as it would appear.

"She's pretty enough to be," Lawrence said softly.

Janie sat up. "Don't say that, Lawrence. Don't even think it."

"Why?" Lawrence sat in the chair opposite and put his chin in his hand. "Are you jealous?"

"Of someone who can't even make a cup of tea?" Janie forced a laugh past the heat that rose in her throat. "No."

"And here I thought you were fishing for compliments." Lawrence sat back and stretched his legs out. His foot nearly touched hers.

"You're fishing for something else if you make comments like that." Janie stood, but couldn't quite turn away from the footman's smile.

"And what might that be?" Lawrence set his hands behind his head. He'd taken his coat off, and the fabric of his shirt tightened over his arms and beneath his waistcoat.

"Dismissal," Janie said, gathering up the teacups. If Lawrence was right, kitchen maids were the wickedest creatures on earth; Janie felt she never had a chance to rest. "Lady Diane doesn't allow flirting."

Lawrence moved to help her. "With Lady Charlotte?" he whispered. He was so close she smelled soap and coconut.

"With anyone." Janie moved away. Janie had only gotten her position as second kitchen maid because the previous girl had been caught kissing the chauffeur.

The chauffeur, of course, had stayed on. *So hard to find a good driver.*

"Then she should have only female staff, like her sister." Lawrence followed Janie back to the kitchen, where Harry was still fiddling with the flue of the second oven. Mid-afternoon was the one time the kitchen was quiet. Briefly.

"Lady Beatrice only hires women?" Janie asked, putting the cups into the sink for Mollie.

"It's cheaper." Lawrence shrugged.

"But she's richer than Croesus," Janie said. "She could hire anyone she wants."

"Maybe she's like the rest of the aristocracy and only pretends to be rich," Harry said, his voice echoing up the chimney.

"All I know is what Lady Beatrice's self-righteous lady's maid told me," Lawrence said. Again he came a little too close for comfort. "She said they didn't need men."

Janie felt like a mouse facing a cobra. Mesmerized. Really, Lawrence's smile was bewitching. And dangerous.

Janie struggled to raise an eyebrow. "So she didn't submit to your charms."

"Not yet," Lawrence purred. "But they all do eventually."

He seemed utterly aware of the power his blue eyes had over her.

Janie turned to stir the consommé simmering on the stove to cover her discomposure. She liked bantering with Lawrence, and she liked the attention, but she was pretty sure he wouldn't be worth losing her job over.

Harry climbed out from behind the second oven, dripping soot and rattling tools.

"Would you ever work in an all-women household?" he asked Janie.

"Lady Beatrice's maid did say she's looking for a cook." Lawrence dipped a finger in the consommé and licked it.

"I'm just the second kitchen maid," Janie said, pushing him away with her shoulder. "I've nowhere near the experience."

"Maybe she'll steal your mother, then." Lawrence winked.

Janie felt the foundation of her existence rock just a little.

"Out with you," she said with a weak laugh. "I've work to do. Unlike some people."

A bell rang in the hall and Lawrence tilted his head to listen to it. The bell rang again. "We've all got work to do,

Janie. Lady Diane needs me in her sitting room and I'm willing to bet that means tea. And perhaps some of those coconut biscuits you made earlier." He flashed a grin before leaving the kitchen, heading for the footman's closet and the stairs up to the marble hall.

"I hope that lady's maid stays away from him," Janie murmured.

"It seems no one is immune to his charms," Harry said acidly, wrapping his tools up in a cloth.

Janie shot him a look. "Anyone would think you're jealous, Harry Peasgood."

Harry stretched his arms. "Me?" he said. "Jealous? Of a tall and devastatingly handsome man who can already see every rung of the ladder to his future? Second footman. Head footman. Butler. He's set for life."

"You *are* jealous." And after all that talk about being an engineer and going to America.

"Only of the devastatingly handsome part." Harry followed Lawrence's path out of the kitchen, and when Janie went to clean the soot from under the stove, she discovered he'd already done it.

She took a cup of tea out to her mother, who sat on an upturned barrel in the courtyard gateway, looking out over the trees. The gate provided minimal shade, and Mrs.

Seward's starch cap drooped to one side. Janie couldn't help noticing that beneath it, her mother's brown hair had begun to gray.

"I should be inside starting dinner, not having a second cuppa," Mrs. Seward said, but took the tea, anyway.

"It's the roast tonight?" Janie asked, leaning against the other side of the gate, the rough stone digging into her shoulder blade through the thin cotton of her dress. She loved discussing the menus with her mother. Talking about how the fish needed to complement the main course, how a cream soup couldn't be served before salmon, or how a fruit dessert could lighten the palate after a heavy meal.

"Change in plan, my dear," Mrs. Seward said, absently sipping her tea. "Lady Beatrice brought chili peppers — imported from India. We're making curry."

"Do we know how to make curry?" Janie asked, and didn't add the question, *And will Lady Diane eat it?* If Her Ladyship called kedgeree foreign, what would she think of the Indian chilies?

"I've done it before," Mrs. Seward said quietly, and looked out over the distant hills. "Isn't it beautiful?"

Janie decided to let Lady Diane worry about the curry and took a moment to breathe in the scents of warm grass and dry leaves and the faintest hint of the lake in the distance.

"Why did you leave?" she asked her mother. Janie knew she'd been born at The Manor. She knew her parents had left shortly after. But she couldn't imagine doing it herself.

"It was your father." Mrs. Seward's eyes sharpened, and she downed the rest of her tea in one gulp, wincing from the heat.

"He didn't want to stay?" Janie pursued.

"Lady Diane didn't want the rest of the servants getting any ideas. She doesn't want her servants getting married. Having children."

Janie nodded. The rules had become stricter in the sixteen years since her birth. Now a kiss would get you fired without reference.

"Besides," her mother said, more quietly, "I wanted to be able to raise you myself."

Again, Janie held her tongue. Because that wasn't what happened. Her coachman father had decided to join the Army. And the better life he promised had become a broken one, with Mrs. Seward working at one country house after another and Janie just one more mouth to feed on her uncle's farm.

"Well," she said instead, "we're together now. And we're here."

Mrs. Seward nodded. "But maybe not for long."

"What do you mean?" Fear grabbed her chest like a vise, making it almost impossible to breathe.

"It may all come to nothing." Mrs. Seward didn't look at her, just stood and turned back to the kitchen.

"What may come to nothing?" Janie managed to squeeze the words past the anxiety in her throat.

"I've been offered another position." Mrs. Seward walked down the basement steps and stopped at the dresser just inside the kitchen door to pull out a clean apron and cap.

Janie couldn't believe she was being so casual. That she had dropped this bomb into Janie's lap and wouldn't even acknowledge that Janie's world was falling apart with the explosion of it.

"Where?" she gasped. "With whom? Doing what?"

But an answer came to her immediately. Lawrence had said Lady Beatrice wanted a cook.

"*Shhh*," Mrs. Seward said. "If Lady Diane even gets a hint of this, I will be out on my ear, do you hear me?"

"It sounds like you're going anyway," Janie snapped. "Why should you care?"

Mrs. Seward turned to face her, fists on her hips.

"There's no need to be like that, my girl."

Janie felt a gush of remorse — even shame — but hardened herself against it. She settled her mouth into a firm line.

"And when were you going to tell me?" she asked. "When we left? Or when you left me behind?"

Janie couldn't decide which would be worse.

"You're nearly grown, Janie Seward," her mother said sharply. "And you already know how the world works. I go where the work is."

"There's work *here*."

"There's more than just work here, Janie," her mother said. "There are memories. I never should have come back."

Janie forced herself to believe she didn't care about her mother's memories. She cared about her own. Life at The Manor had provided her with memories she wanted to keep. With friends, like Harry.

And Lawrence.

"And what about me?" Janie couldn't stop her voice from breaking. "Did you not concern yourself at all with me? With how I would feel about this?"

She'd already spent so much time away from her mother. She couldn't imagine spending more. But by the same token, she couldn't leave the only home she'd ever known. The kitchen was her sanctuary.

Mrs. Seward unfolded her arms and wrapped them around Janie. She smoothed the back of her cap and pressed Janie's face into her shoulder.

"Of course I'd never want to leave you," she said. But Janie heard what she didn't say. That leaving her might be necessary, whether she wanted it or not.

# Chapter 5

Charlotte knew enough not to watch every move Lawrence made while he was serving the tea. But she did see the fabric of his deep blue livery jacket slide across his shoulders. And catch the smile he flashed at her before he left.

Lady Diane sat beneath the great north-facing window with her back to the sky and the hills, only her head inclined over the desk where she sat composing invitations to a Saturday-to-Monday house party.

The rest of her mother's body was so upright. So stiff.

"Is Aunt Beatrice going to join us?" Charlotte sat up straighter and tried to incline her head the way her mother did. When a twinge shot up the back of her neck, she rubbed it and sighed. She would never meet her mother's full approval.

"Don't sigh, Charlotte, it's very unbecoming." Lady Diane

didn't look up from her desk. "My sister has gone out walking. Why she doesn't *ride*, I've no idea."

It seemed *no one* could meet her full approval. So why try?

Charlotte slouched back over her worn copy of *The Return of Sherlock Holmes*. She thought she might go mad. Her mother had requested her presence all day long. First, to go over the long and tedious weekend menus. Lady Diane kept going on about Lord Broadhurst's elegant taste in cuisine and how important it was for Charlotte to understand. Really, who cared if one had a cream-based pudding or a fruit-based one?

Then all afternoon was spent visiting neighbors. Leaving a calling card at one house, not even getting out of the green Daimler motorcar at another. Every visit strictly defined by social status and tradition.

And now tea.

Charlotte looked to her book for inspiration. Holmes and Watson always found a way out of a situation. Though even in her wildest imaginings, Charlotte couldn't picture herself climbing over a garden wall to escape her mother.

She could imagine Janie doing it. During her few moments alone, Charlotte had even begun a story in which Janie was an adventuress, facing valiantly most dire of situations.

That's why she needed Janie to help her find out about Aunt Beatrice.

Charlotte set her book down on the little side table with its spindly, decorated legs. She rose from the shiny damask of the upholstered chair and brushed her skirts.

"Mother," she said, and cleared her throat when her mother didn't look up.

"What a horrid noise, Charlotte. Really."

Lady Diane's eyes remained on her letter, but at least Charlotte knew she was listening.

"Mother, I'm going to go . . ." Charlotte's nerve left her. ". . . for a walk."

Lady Diane looked up at that. "I don't think that's a good idea."

"I'd like some fresh air."

Lady Diane frowned. Lately, she seemed to frown perpetually.

"You don't want to turn a dreadful brown before the shooting party. Lord Broadhurst will be here."

*All the more reason to turn a dreadful brown,* Charlotte thought. If it might convince Andrew Broadhurst she wasn't marriage material, she would spend all day lying on a chaise with her face upturned.

"Of course, Mother," she said. "I promise I won't let the sun touch my face." She neglected to say this was because she wouldn't be leaving the house.

Lady Diane looked ready to argue, but an echo of voices from the marble hall interrupted them. Lawrence strode into the room and bowed.

"Your Ladyship, Lady Beatrice has returned from her walk and requested tea."

Lady Diane actually smiled at the footman. Charlotte was shocked. It seemed no one was immune to Lawrence's charms.

"She may join me in here, Lawrence," Lady Diane said evenly, and then turned her smile on Charlotte, but it quickly disappeared. "Now don't sulk, Charlotte. Go out. Wear a hat. And don't leave the garden."

Charlotte silently cursed her poor timing. "I can stay in if you'd rather." Even with her mother there, she could surely find out a few things about Beatrice if they were able to be in the same room together.

"No, fresh air is good for you. Go now."

End of discussion.

Charlotte ran up the stairs, hoping to catch her aunt in the hall, but all the doors were closed. So she continued on down the servants' staircase. She didn't have a lamp or a candle, so she left the door open to let the hall light spill down the stairs.

The kitchen was like what Charlotte imagined a Turkish bath would be. Steam hung in the air, and tepid water dripped from the ceiling. Mrs. Seward and Janie were bathed in sweat, their aprons limp despite the starch and their drab gray dresses spotted with water and grease.

"I told you to open the windows!" Mrs. Seward sighed, wiping the back of a hand over her forehead.

"I did," Janie muttered, not looking at her mother.

Charlotte took in the entire scene. The steam came from the scullery as well as from the kettle and other pots bubbling on the coal-fired stove. One end of the scarred kitchen table was a mess of sticky flour, and the other end hosted a pile of brightly colored vegetables, some of which Charlotte didn't even recognize. Janie stood over them, looking overwhelmed.

Charlotte reconsidered her lie to her mother and decided that perhaps a walk would be the best thing for her. She was unlikely to be welcomed here.

She turned into the passageway and ran immediately into Lawrence. The jacket and waistcoat of his livery were unbuttoned. When he spotted her, the tray of newly polished silver he carried tipped dangerously, sending a saltcellar and two candlesticks crashing to the floor.

"*Now* what?" Mrs. Seward bellowed from the kitchen.

"Lady Charlotte." Lawrence hesitated, trying to balance the tray on one arm while he buttoned his waistcoat with the other hand. Trying not to stare, Charlotte crouched down to pick up the saltcellar. One side was dented.

"Oh, laws."

Charlotte looked up to see Mrs. Seward smoothing her apron and straightening her cap. She reached for the tray.

"Get away with you, Lawrence. Wandering around half-dressed. What were you thinking?"

Lawrence raised an eyebrow at Mrs. Seward — or was it at Janie just behind her? — and grinned. He bowed to Charlotte and spun on his heel to retreat to the butler's pantry.

"Gracious." Mrs. Seward turned back to the steam of the kitchen. "Janie, pick up the silver. It will have to be done again."

Charlotte held out the saltcellar mutely. She hadn't meant to cause more work. More trouble.

"I didn't . . ." she began, but had no idea how to continue. The kitchen looked alarmingly busy. But Janie had said that gossip traveled faster than fire downstairs. Surely Charlotte would be able to find something out.

"What can we do for you, Lady Charlotte?" Mrs. Seward asked, handing Janie the tray, which wobbled again. Charlotte's eyes widened in horror. It must be very heavy. And a tiny thing like Janie seemed unlikely to be able to handle it.

Janie glowered at her.

"I just . . ." Charlotte stood up straighter, trying to be more like her mother. "I wondered how things were going." That sounded stupid. "For dinner."

Mrs. Seward stopped moving for a moment — something she didn't seem to do very often. Then she sighed almost imperceptibly.

"Did your mother have any late requests, Lady Charlotte?"

The question was posed graciously. As if there were nothing Mrs. Seward would like better than to make one more dish.

"No!" Charlotte stuttered. "I just . . . wondered."

Mother and daughter exchanged a look, and Janie went back to her vegetables. She picked up a tiny red fruit by its stem and looked at it dubiously.

"What are you making?" Charlotte asked, watching her.

"Curry." Mrs. Seward retreated to the other end of the table and swept the clots of flour into a bucket and then put the bucket under the table. Everything was done with effortlessness and grace — like a dance.

Charlotte couldn't imagine her mother ordering curry. Something so . . . foreign. Other people had curry. Sometimes even for breakfast. But her mother barely tolerated kedgeree. Charlotte took a step into the steaming kitchen. The steam smelled like laundry and tea and meat pie from luncheon. Not like another country.

"From India?" she asked, moving so her back was up against the wall. She didn't want to risk getting in the way again.

Mrs. Seward huffed. "Your aunt requested it."

Charlotte didn't have time to ask any questions because a boy stepped in through the door carrying two pairs of shoes in his right hand and one in his left. He wasn't terribly tall, but had broad shoulders that stretched the fabric of his cambric shirt. His light brown hair was astonishingly curly, but it looked soft. The kind you'd want to touch. He walked up behind Janie, looking avidly between Janie's face and the little fruit she held between her thumb and forefinger.

"So, have you eaten one yet?"

He tucked the pair of shoes under his right arm and reached his left hand out. Janie snatched the fruit away.

"Your hands are filthy, Harry," she chided. "Covered in boot black."

He turned away, lining up the shoes next to the scullery door, and went to the sink beneath the window.

"I thought you'd give it a go before I dared you," he said, washing his hands, his voice quick with gaiety. To Charlotte it sounded a little false. Like he was covering up his embarrassment.

"Because we all know how well things go for me when I do one of your dares, Harry Peasgood." Janie barely looked up from the other vegetables she was slicing.

Charlotte couldn't believe how casual Janie was. She

didn't struggle to think of something clever to say or start a conversation that the boy could dominate. She just . . . spoke.

"The dive off the ha-ha was not my fault," Harry said, scrubbing between his fingers with the lye soap. "I just said I had never seen anyone go off it headfirst. I never imagined you'd think to do it."

"That was a dare?" Charlotte blurted.

Harry turned around and nearly dropped the soap. He juggled it deftly and turned to place it on the edge of the sink, rinsing his hands before turning around again.

"Lady Charlotte." Harry's voice was neutral. No more teasing.

"It was a mistake," Janie said. Then she frowned and held up a little fruit, inspecting it. It looked wrinkled — like it was past its prime — and was a deep red, almost maroon color.

"What is that?" Charlotte asked, taking a step toward Janie and pointing at the little fruit.

"It's a chili pepper."

Charlotte took a step closer. Glanced at Harry.

"Why is he daring you to eat it?" she asked.

"*He* is Harry Peasgood, your hall boy," Janie said. "And he's been daring me to do things for the four years I've been here."

Charlotte heard the distrust in Janie's voice as well as the impertinence. In a way, she felt she deserved it. After all, hadn't she gotten Janie's name wrong? Why did she ever think Janie would want to help her?

Charlotte glanced at Harry again. She knew the hall boy cleaned the boots and kept the gun room tidy and slept in the hall to deter intruders. But like the other downstairs servants, he was hardly ever visible to the family. He looked to be about a year older than she was. He had a crooked smile and eyes almost the same color as his hair.

"Hello, Harry," she said quietly. And then spontaneously held out her hand. They all stared at it for a moment before Harry grinned at her and shook it swiftly.

"The chili pepper is an acquired taste," he said, plucking the thing out of Janie's hand. "They say in India people eat them all the time. In everything. That they stimulate the appetite in the heat."

Charlotte took another step closer and narrowed her eyes a little.

"But why are you daring Janie to eat it?"

"Because it's meant to set your tongue on fire," Janie said, pulling the pepper back out of Harry's hand and putting it down on the table. She picked up a little paring knife and deftly removed the stem.

"Really?" Charlotte asked. "Is that what makes Indian food so spicy?"

Janie nodded and slit the little fruit down one side, getting ready to chop it.

"May I try?" Charlotte asked, and reached out a hand. Janie backed up, holding the knife in front of her.

"Don't you know better than to stick your finger under a chopping knife?" she snapped.

"Janie Mae!" Mrs. Seward cried, and the room again dissolved into stillness and silence.

"No." Charlotte took a step backward. "No, I guess I don't. But I'd like to learn."

The other three stared at her like she had just come in from India herself. Like she was something foreign and indescribable.

"Well, then." The voice came from behind her, deep and vibrating. Charlotte turned as Lawrence walked into the kitchen, his buttons all done up and his jacket brushed. "I say we should all take a chance, then, don't you think?"

He took Janie's wrist and slid the knife's handle out of her grip. He sliced the pepper into four even pieces, left the knife on the table, and placed all four pieces in his palm. He held out his open hand to Charlotte first.

She hesitated. He had never handed her anything other than on a tray before. And never without gloves. She looked up to catch Janie watching, one eyebrow arched.

This was a test. Of her fortitude. But also of her ability to disregard the wall that separated mistress from servant. To prove that she was willing to learn.

Gingerly, Charlotte took one of the pieces from him, her skin touching his. She held the pepper between her finger and thumb, and looked up at his face. His blue eyes lingered on her just a moment too long before he turned to offer a piece to Janie, and finally to Harry. The hall boy hesitated.

"'Once more unto the breach'?" Lawrence asked, holding up a piece of pepper.

"Once *more*, Lawrence?" Harry asked, his voice dry and a little sarcastic. But he took it.

"To coin a phrase."

Lawrence turned again to Charlotte.

In fact, all of them were staring at her. As the person with most precedence, she should eat first. Perhaps this was what it felt like to be dared to do something. Charlotte looked down at the pepper in her fingers. The skin was almost waxy, the interior a lighter color, moist and threaded with little creases, speckled by tiny seeds.

She thought of what Janie had said, that the pepper set the tongue on fire. Her courage left her and she stared helplessly at the kitchen maid, hoping for reprieve.

"'Cry God for Harry, England, and Saint George!'" Janie said and dropped the piece of pepper onto her tongue. Janie's eyes watered, but she raised an eyebrow at Charlotte. A challenge.

Lawrence laughed and followed suit and Harry close after.

"Water," Harry gasped and turned to the sink behind him, placing his entire mouth under the spigot. Janie laughed, her cheeks red and the tears streaming freely down her face.

Lawrence hiccuped, his lips pressed tightly together, his eyes squeezed shut. He hiccuped again.

Charlotte knew she'd never be accepted unless she tried this. She'd never be an adventurer — or even a writer — if she didn't do things that frightened her. She had to prove her mettle if she ever wanted to ask Janie for help.

Charlotte put the piece of pepper in her mouth and chewed until it seemed the very sun of India burned bright upon her tongue.

Janie handed her a glass of milk and raised one of her own in a silent toast.

Charlotte smiled through the fire. "The game's afoot," she said.

She had passed the test.

# Chapter 6

Janie sat with Harry on an empty crate in the kitchen courtyard. It was just gone ten o'clock at night, but light still streaked the sky, and the heat of the day radiated off the cobblestones.

Janie leaned slightly to the right, resting on Harry's shoulder so he could take some of the weight off her aching bones. He shifted a little, tilting his head back, his face to the newly visible stars.

Janie closed her eyes, listening as someone picked out a tune on the piano in the servants' hall. It stuttered to a stop and then began again, and she recognized Lawrence's baritone singing Harry Champion's music hall hit, "I'm Henery the Eighth, I Am." Making Sarah the housemaid laugh.

"Don't you think it's odd that Lady Charlotte came to the kitchen today?" Janie asked.

Harry shifted again. "She said she wanted to learn." He didn't take his eyes off the stars.

Janie turned her head slightly, looking at his profile. She could see the freckles scattered across his cheekbones.

"But why?" she asked, watching his eyes watch the sky. "Do you think she gets a thrill out of going slumming?" She hoped he would disagree with her. She was beginning to like Lady Charlotte. Janie smiled, thinking of the look on the other girl's face when the fire of the chili hit her tongue.

Harry finally turned to look at her and smiled back, his face mere inches from hers. "Maybe she just thinks we're interesting people."

"She's got a whole party of people coming on Thursday."

"Even the aristocracy gets bored. Must be why they hunt and shoot. If you can't entertain yourself, go kill something."

"But Lady Charlotte doesn't shoot."

"So she comes into the kitchen instead. It's just as dangerous, Janie, with you there."

Janie stuck out her tongue.

"And what's she thinking, making eyes at Lawrence?" she mused out loud.

Harry moved away, the gap of summer air not nearly as warm as his arm had been.

"That's not the sort of accusation you want to be making too loudly, Janie," he said. "You could just be nice to her. Her brothers are all out in the real world. She's probably lonely." He paused. "Maybe she needs a friend."

"She's got the Caldwell girl."

"You know what most of these people are like — rules come first and people last." Harry turned back to the stars. "It doesn't hurt to show a little compassion."

"Are you trying to say I don't care about people?" Janie said. "That I'm not compassionate?"

"It's not what I was saying at all." Harry refused to rise to her bait. "It seems that there's something you're not telling me. That you have other reasons for not wanting her around."

"I just don't like change."

"Change is inevitable, Janie," Harry said, rising and brushing the dust off of his trousers. "It's coming whether you like it or not."

Janie couldn't look at him. Maybe he was right, but that didn't mean she had to accept it. She desperately wanted to tell him about her mother's job offer, but couldn't. Talking about it would make it seem too real.

Lawrence finished his song with a flourish and a single extended note, Sarah giggling the entire time. Janie sighed.

"Time to check the hall and front door," Harry said, and left without looking back.

Janie stood, took off her apron, and put it in to soak in the laundry. She stepped into the kitchen, breathing in the scents of soap and coal and lemon and the lingering odors of curry. The table was scrubbed and laid out with the tools for breakfast. Music came again from the servants' hall — a ragtime waltz. Someone would be dancing.

A movement at the door caught her eye.

Lady Charlotte stood, perched on her toes, one hand on the door frame. She was looking toward the servants' hall, her head cocked to the side, listening to the music. Her hair was down around her shoulders — a flood of that thick, straight hair. Like water, it was. So different from Janie's hair, which tended to frizz in the humidity like her mother's.

Lady Charlotte wore an ill-fitting traveling dress, hastily buttoned. Janie wondered with horror if the girl planned to run away.

"Can I help, Lady Charlotte?" she asked. And realized, in light of her previous thought, that she sounded a bit inconsiderate, so she amended herself. "Is there anything I can do for you?"

"I . . . I heard music." Lady Charlotte blushed a little and slipped into the kitchen, backing up against the wall. Like she didn't want to be seen.

"Sometimes at night, someone plays the piano," Janie said. "They move the table to the side and dance."

"Dancing? With each other?" Lady Charlotte looked like she was about to go investigate.

A surge of fear caught Janie in the chest. If Lady Diane found out, would she put a stop to the nightly dancing? If she found out that Janie had told Lady Charlotte, would Lady Diane shoot the messenger?

"After all the work is done," Janie said quickly. "And nothing inappropriate."

"Do you dance?" Lady Charlotte turned back to her, and again Janie saw the look of excitement fill her eyes.

"I like the hesitation waltz," Janie replied.

"Hesitation?"

"It's new. Instead of turning with every measure, you take an entire three beats to brush forward or back or to the side. Your feet don't move much." She could see Lady Charlotte didn't know what she was talking about. "Watch."

Janie put her arms around an imaginary partner. "One, two, three," she counted with the music, spinning around the kitchen in a normal waltz step. Then she came to the next measure and slid her right foot to the side for almost the bar, pausing minutely to bring her left in before sliding the left to the side for the next count.

"But that's easy," Lady Charlotte said, stepping farther into the room.

Janie thought about what Harry had said. About Lady Charlotte needing a friend.

"Come and try it," Janie said. She held her arms out.

"With you?" Lady Charlotte asked.

"I don't see anyone else here."

Lady Charlotte grinned and put a hand on Janie's shoulder. "You're a bit shorter than what I'm used to."

Janie laughed. "The housemaids always dance together down here. There aren't enough eligible men to go around." She almost bit her tongue to retract the statement. It sounded like she was looking for a boyfriend.

But Lady Charlotte nodded. "I know exactly what you mean. The last dance I went to, I had to sit on the side the entire time. Mother would only let me dance with the boys I know because I'm not out in society yet. I danced twice with Andrew Broadhurst."

"Lord Broadhurst is very good-looking," Janie said, stepping into the waltz and dragging Lady Charlotte with her. Then she realized they were both trying not to lead, so she changed her stance and nodded, and they started again. This time with Janie leading.

"Is he?" Lady Charlotte mused.

Janie thought of the young man she'd seen a few times, walking from car to house or out in the garden. And once even in the kitchen, asking her mother about the cakes. He was tall and slender, with strikingly dark brown eyes.

"I think so," she said. "Definitely dance-worthy."

Lady Charlotte shook her head. "Dull as a doormat, I'm afraid."

"Do you know him well?"

"Not very. All he ever talks about is the weather. Or food."

Janie bristled a little. "There's more to food than just eating it, you know. Sometimes people aren't what you think they are at first."

"Oh, I didn't mean to offend you!" Lady Charlotte stopped moving, and Janie trod on her calfskin boot, leaving a dark smudge on the pale toe.

"I'm so sorry, Lady Charlotte," Janie said quickly, and started to move away. "Please let me get something to clean that up."

"It was my fault." Lady Charlotte put a hand on Janie's arm to stop her.

Janie blinked in surprise and turned to face her.

"You're right," Lady Charlotte said. "You can't really *know* someone until you know more about them, can you?" She paused.

Janie nodded cautiously.

"Well, my aunt Beatrice," Lady Charlotte went on. "I don't really know her, you see? I've never really met her. She's lived abroad for so long. And I . . . I want to know why she's here."

There was something Lady Charlotte wasn't saying, Janie was sure of that. But she nodded again, hoping it would all become clear.

"Mother doesn't want me to spend any time with her." Lady Charlotte was speaking faster. "With Aunt Beatrice, that is. And I'd like to know why. I'd like to know *her*; she's such an adventuress and all. But I can't. Mother insists that I spend all my time with the guests at the shooting party. With Lord Broadhurst." Lady Charlotte pulled a face but quickly altered it. "Whom I'm going to try to get to know better, as per your suggestion." She smiled.

"People *are* surprising," Janie agreed.

"But I was hoping that I could find out more about Aunt Beatrice."

"So talk to her," Janie suggested with a shrug.

"That's just it; I can't. Mother won't let me out of her sight."

"You're here now." Janie didn't know why Lady Charlotte was telling her all of this. And was even less sure she wanted to know.

"And Aunt Beatrice is asleep. But you said . . ." Lady Charlotte paused. "You said servants know things."

Janie waited for her to continue, but Lady Charlotte just bit her lower lip expectantly. As if anticipating some kind of response.

"I'm not sure I entirely understand," Janie said.

"You won't really spy on her or anything."

"Spy?"

"Nothing so underhanded or immoral. It's not like I want you to go through her papers or anything."

"So what exactly are you asking me to do?" Janie asked cautiously. Because there wasn't much she *could* do. She couldn't go upstairs and had yet even to catch a glimpse of Lady Beatrice. "Dig up gossip?"

"Maybe just . . . listen."

"And repeat it to you."

Janie thought of Lawrence and the information he'd extracted from Beatrice's lady's maid. A staff entirely of women. Janie might not be able to find out information on her own, but she certainly knew who could.

Lady Charlotte bit her lip. "I just need something, Janie. *Anything*. I want to know who she is. And why she's here."

Suddenly, Janie realized that she needed to know exactly the same thing. If her mother really was planning to take a position on Lady Beatrice's staff, Janie had to find out about it. Soon.

So she could prevent it.

And if she discovered any dark secrets about Beatrice, perhaps she could convince her mother not to leave. And everything would go back to the way it had always been.

Janie nodded.

"You'll do it?" Lady Charlotte asked.

Janie froze. And nodded again.

And she pretended to smile when Lady Charlotte squealed in delight.

"We'll need to find a way to get you upstairs," Lady Charlotte said.

Janie's guard went up. "I can listen perfectly well downstairs."

"But . . . there may be more you can do upstairs."

"I thought you didn't want me to spy."

"Oh, I don't." Lady Charlotte looked aghast, but bit her lip again.

Janie waited. She was going to make Lady Charlotte say it. And then refuse her to her face.

Lady Charlotte looked down. Her right hand squeezed her left so hard, her knuckles turned white.

"I just . . ." she said, and paused. "It's difficult for me to get away. From Mother. And if you could come upstairs, we could . . . talk. Because I'd like to get to know you, too."

Janie again thought about Charlotte needing a friend.

"All right," she finally said.

And regretted it immediately.

# Chapter 7

Charlotte almost swept Janie into another waltz, right there in the kitchen. She was making a difference in her own life. She was making things *happen*. She felt she could make *anything* happen.

"Come to my room at three o'clock," Charlotte told Janie. "Every day. No matter what."

"Even if there's nothing to tell you?"

If Charlotte didn't know better, she'd think Janie looked a little scared.

"No matter what."

The kitchen maid bit her lip and looked away.

"Is there a problem?" Charlotte asked.

Janie shook her head sharply and then looked up, her hazel eyes troubled.

"I don't know which is your room."

Charlotte relaxed. "It's the second on the left. From the servants' stairs."

Janie nodded, still frowning. Charlotte waited.

"What if I get caught?" Janie finally asked.

"You won't." Charlotte smiled. Almost laughed. "No one's upstairs at that time of day. And certainly no one will be near my room." She paused, every trace of laughter suddenly erased. "I think they stuck me there so they can forget about me."

She sagged against the wall, depleted. She was deluding herself, thinking she could make a difference.

A flash of imagination crossed her mind. An Italian count. A daring escape.

And then, almost as if she had conjured him up with her very thoughts, Lawrence appeared in the doorway. He had taken off his livery jacket and waistcoat, his white shirt in bright contrast to his dark hair, his white tie undone and hanging loose against his unbuttoned collar.

"Janie," he called. "Come and have a dance. Harry says you promised him, but I've come to claim you."

Charlotte felt a stab beneath her rib cage — half jealousy, half longing. She wished she lived in a world where someone could casually ask for a dance, not a world of prescription and formal introductions. She wished she could talk to boys like Janie could — like they were equals. She wished she could discuss chili peppers and not the weather.

She wished Lawrence hadn't asked Janie to dance.

But Janie wasn't responding. She didn't jump straight into Lawrence's arms. She didn't even smile. She stepped away a tiny bit, so her back was against the great oak table, and her fingers gripped the edge of it. Her eyes darted once to Charlotte and then to Lawrence.

He caught the glance and turned. And his smile grew even wider when he saw Charlotte, making her fingers tingle and her heart hammer high in her throat.

"Lady Charlotte," he said with a bow. He didn't scramble to retie his tie. He didn't run in search of his waistcoat. He just straightened up and smiled again.

"How kind of you to grace us with your presence," he said, and Charlotte found herself wishing he were less formal. That he could call her Charlotte, and drop the "Lady."

"I was . . ." Charlotte found herself more tongue-tied than usual.

"I was just showing Lady Charlotte the hesitation waltz," Janie interjected, stepping forward. "She heard the music and came down the back stairs."

Lawrence raised an eyebrow at Janie and then turned to Charlotte.

"And what did you think, Lady Charlotte?"

"It's different." Charlotte paused and then grinned. "It made it easier to navigate around the table." She was delighted with herself for saying something so blithely. An echo of the banter Janie seemed so comfortable with.

"Very different from what you're used to. In a ballroom." Lawrence's expression didn't change, but Janie frowned. Charlotte realized she sounded a little spoiled and wished she had said nothing at all.

"And we had trouble figuring out who would lead," Janie said, pointing to the black mark on Charlotte's toe. "I'm afraid Lady Charlotte's shoes have suffered for it."

Lawrence laughed and Charlotte felt again a little stab of jealousy. Until he turned those eyes on her. And it was like she was the only person in the room.

"I know how to lead," he said. "Would you like to dance, Lady Charlotte?" And he held out his hand to her.

He wore no gloves. Charlotte looked down at her own hands. Neither did she.

This night wasn't going the way she'd imagined. Her plan had been to talk to Janie. She'd imagined herself sneaking back up the stairs, not seen by any of the other servants. Certainly not seen in her hastily donned traveling dress, having tried — and failed — to lace her own corset.

She hadn't imagined herself dancing with the footman.

But she found herself wanting to.

Janie stepped between them. For a second, Charlotte thought the kitchen maid was going to whisk Lawrence off into the dance herself. Instead, Janie took Charlotte's hand in hers.

"It's all right," Janie said, placing Charlotte's hand in Lawrence's. "He won't bite. At least not during a waltz."

When Lawrence stepped closer, Charlotte expected something extraordinary to happen. She expected thunder to sound. Or her mother to enter the room and scream the house down.

But all she felt was Lawrence's confidence — his fingers gentle, but slightly rough at the edges, and the strength of his grasp.

When she felt his other hand on her waist, she was suddenly — painfully — aware that she hadn't tightened her corset. That her skirt was merely pinned closed. That she could feel her clothes moving against her skin. She'd danced with boys before, of course. Under the watchful eye of her mother and the entire aristocratic circle of Kent and Sussex.

She'd danced with her brothers and the local landowners and her father. She'd danced with Andrew Broadhurst.

But Andrew held her hand lightly, his fingers barely touching her waist as he methodically led her through the dance.

Lawrence held her hand firmly, his touch on her lower back sure and present, his fingers pressing her skin through the thin linen of her traveling jacket every time he steered her in another direction. Lawrence danced like he *felt* the music. He held her like he was sure she wouldn't break.

He waltzed her around the table as if they were in an uncrowded ballroom, each turn bringing her another glimpse of the stove, the window, the sink, Janie. She had to move exactly as he wanted, follow his rhythm, his guidance.

This wasn't a showy dance with quick turns. It didn't cover a lot of ground. It wasn't one where the girl could draw attention to the drape of her skirts or traverse an entire ballroom. It was intimate. Close.

Delicious.

She was just getting the hang of it — the music building into the final measures — when Lawrence stepped her into a spin. She turned beneath his arm, looking up into his face. His hand was light on hers against her stomach. His breath whispered on her cheek.

Suddenly, Janie pushed between them, clipping Charlotte's hip on the edge of the table and nearly sending her sprawling.

"What the bloody letter, Janie?" Lawrence yelped, stumbling away from them.

"Language, Lawrence," another voice said.

Everything in the room stopped. Mrs. Griffiths, the housekeeper, stood in the doorway.

Charlotte braced herself on the table. Out of the corner of her eye, she saw Lawrence buttoning his collar.

"Lady Charlotte," Mrs. Griffiths said coolly. She was the picture of deference, but her eyes held censure. Behind her, Charlotte caught a glimpse of Sarah the housemaid.

Charlotte looked around the room, terrified. Hoping for rescue. When she saw her expression mirrored in theirs, she realized Janie and Lawrence could get into much more serious trouble than she could. So she stepped forward.

"I was just going, Mrs. Griffiths."

Mrs. Griffiths narrowed her eyes. "Sarah, would you accompany Lady Charlotte to her room, please?" The housekeeper's Welsh lilt grew more pronounced when she was angry.

"Janie can take me, Mrs. Griffiths," Charlotte said quickly.

"A *kitchen* maid upstairs in the bedrooms?"

The housekeeper's voice conveyed all anyone needed to know. All Charlotte needed to know. No wonder Janie was afraid to go upstairs. No wonder she was afraid of getting caught. Charlotte wondered if Janie would come the next day at three o'clock. She wondered if she had made a mistake in asking.

Janie didn't move, but Sarah stepped aside to let Charlotte pass, one hand guarding her from the flame of the candle she held.

As she walked through the kitchen doorway, Charlotte threw one last glance at Lawrence over her shoulder.

But his eyes didn't meet hers. So she walked up the stairs silently, the shadows of the candle following her.

# Chapter 8

Janie felt for the floor with her toes. The stuffiness of her attic room hadn't abated much, even with the window open, and she felt a little queasy. She leaned over and shook Mollie, who snorted and flapped an angry hand and then turned over. Janie knew how she felt.

Two hours of sleep.

Mrs. Griffiths had brought Mr. Foyle, the butler, in. And all of the people still left in the servants' hall. Mollie, Sarah, Tess. Even Lady Beatrice's lady's maid, who had just come down to ask for a needle and thread. Mr. Foyle had lectured them all on the house divisions for over an hour. Respecting the privacy of the family. But also respecting their status.

"Remember your place," he said at last. "Remember your station and never forget it."

Servants. Downstairs.

"Remember that your life here begins and ends with the earl's family. You are only temporary, and they will remain long after you are gone."

Janie knew The Manor wasn't her real home. Not like it was Charlotte's. Her life wasn't a children's story. But when she'd arrived, it had been like something out of Dickens, where a beneficent angel had bestowed upon her everything she'd ever wanted.

Food.

A bed.

Her mother.

A friend.

Janie had Harry. And Charlotte had — what? Money. Comforts. Beautiful dresses. A mother who commanded much and bestowed little. And a room at the end of a long hall, far away from everyone else.

So after Janie woke her mother, fed the servants, cleaned the kitchen, helped prepare luncheon, and cleaned the kitchen *again*, she washed her hands carefully, put on a clean apron and cap, and climbed the back stairs to the second-story landing.

She stopped, one palm flat on the thick, woolly fabric that covered the green door. She didn't have to go. She knew she *shouldn't* go. It was too great a risk.

But Harry's words haunted her. And so did her glimpse of the world abovestairs the day she sneaked Charlotte back to her room.

She wanted to see it again.

Stepping through the door was like entering another country. The carpet beneath her feet was like walking on the thickest of newly mown grass. The electric lights cast glaring halos across the ceiling. The paintings were like great windows to the sky. Or the past. She breathed in the scents of furniture polish and perfume. The odors of affluence.

And silence was the sound of it. No clanging pots or loud voices. No ringing bells. Her feet made no noise as she crept past the first door on the left.

She glanced back once to the servants' stairs. The door had fit back into the wall, the wainscoting and dado rail blending almost seamlessly. Barely visible. As if the downstairs didn't exist.

Or existed only to serve when needed.

Janie stopped outside the second door.

Opposite Charlotte's door was a large painting of a man and a woman. The woman had a band of curls over her forehead and looked straight out of the portrait into the hall. As if she could see Janie's every move. The man had a long face with a pointed beard and a sensuous mouth, his long, dark, curly hair spilling over his shoulders. He looked at the woman as if she were his very life.

Janie turned to Charlotte's door and lifted her hand. Her fingers were red and raw — the skin cracked from scrubbing the copper pots in the scullery because Mollie couldn't get them to Mrs. Seward's standards. So obvious against the clean white elegance of the door.

Janie strengthened her resolve and knocked. The swift motion broke the silence like a thunderclap and pushed the door half-open. Janie caught a glimpse of Charlotte hunched over her desk, scrambling up a sheaf of papers.

Charlotte looked over and Janie dropped her gaze and turned away. She shouldn't be peeking into people's rooms. Like she was really spying.

"Janie!" Even Charlotte was whispering. Janie heard the door open all the way, and Charlotte joined her in the corridor. "You came!"

Janie nodded, her eyes on the painting across the hall.

"Is that . . . ?" Janie asked, gesturing to the canvas.

"A Van Dyck," Charlotte said.

"Charles the First?" Janie said at the same time, and blushed. "I'm afraid I don't know paintings. But I read a book once. About him." She wished she were back in the kitchen. Soufflés and aspics she understood. Kings and Van Dycks made her feet itch.

Charlotte fidgeted for a moment. She felt it, too, Janie could tell. But then she stepped forward and looped her arm through Janie's in a proprietary manner.

"Come in and see my room." Her tone was soothing. Like something one would use on a shifty horse.

The window of Charlotte's room looked out over the patio and the formal garden. And beyond — to the hills and the river. The sun was just beginning to dip toward the west, turning the lake into a dark and mysterious hollow between the hills. It was the same view Janie saw from the kitchen gate every morning. But different. Framed, like a painting.

Sunlight flooded the room. The walls were a lemony yellow, the wainscot a leafy green. Drapes of the same green hung from the giant four-poster bed, the thick velvety counterpane turned down from the white linen of the pillow. The pot of ink on the desk stood open, the top page of the hastily gathered papers covered in curling cursive.

"What do you think?" Charlotte asked. She sounded shy. Nervous.

"It's lovely." Janie's gaze moved involuntarily again to the window. What she wouldn't do to have that view. Her own window opened too high to see out of, just under the rafters, and facing the drive.

"I was just . . ." Charlotte angled her body between Janie and the window. No, not the window. The desk. She kept stealing uneasy glances at the pages lying there.

"Writing?" Janie finished for her.

"It's silly." Charlotte picked at the lace cuff of her peach-colored tea gown. But then she frowned. "No. It's not silly." She looked Janie in the eye. "It's private. And Mother wouldn't approve."

"I'm not supposed to be here, remember?" Janie said. "I won't tell."

"I was afraid you wouldn't come," Charlotte said quickly. "After last night."

"I almost didn't."

Charlotte bit her lip. "I hope I didn't get anyone in trouble."

"You got everyone in trouble." Janie wanted to take back the words as soon as she said them.

Charlotte slapped a hand across her mouth, tears springing to her eyes.

"Oh, no," she said. "What can I do? What can I do to make it better?"

All kinds of solutions came to Janie's mind. *You can be a better mistress than your mother. You can leave us alone.*

"Don't come downstairs anymore." It was exactly what the butler had told them that morning at breakfast. If anyone saw Lady Charlotte in the servants' part of the house, they were to escort her immediately to Mrs. Griffiths, who would take her back upstairs. As if she were a toddler who needed minding.

But Janie couldn't say all of that to Charlotte.

Charlotte sat on the edge of her bed and looked down at her hands clasped on her knees. "That's what my mother said."

Janie swallowed the sour dread that rose in the back of her throat. "Lady Diane knows?"

"Mrs. Griffiths told her. I explained that you didn't know I wasn't supposed to go downstairs. That it wasn't your fault."

Janie frowned. "You're forbidden from going downstairs?" The Manor was Charlotte's home. And even she couldn't venture into parts of it?

"One of Mother's rules. She says . . . she says it will corrupt me."

Janie almost laughed. "Corrupted by spending time with

people who are too busy to eat their meals, and too exhausted to have fun?"

Charlotte looked up. "I had fun last night, Janie. It was the most fun I'd had in months. Except for eating that chili. And putting my toes in the lake."

"So maybe I *am* corrupting you."

"There's got to be more to life than calling cards and charity fetes!" Charlotte cried, standing up and pacing the room from one end to the other. Janie noticed it took at least a dozen strides. Probably more. In her attic room, there was barely enough space to stand between her bed and Mollie's. "There's got to be more than waiting for Andrew bloody Broadhurst to propose."

This time Janie did laugh. "Language, Lady Charlotte."

Charlotte stopped dead in the center of the room, eyes wide. Then she started to laugh, too.

"No wonder Mother has me locked up in my room," she said. "She'll only let me out on my wedding day."

The idea seemed infinitely foreign to Janie. Yet she and Charlotte were the same age. Surely too young to think of marriage.

"Lord Broadhurst is going to propose to you?"

"Mother's been sure of it since I was born, I think. It would be like marrying dry toast. Bland. Boring. Always the same."

"It's nice to know what you can expect," Janie said. "Even dry toast is better than starvation."

Charlotte flopped backward onto her bed.

"But it's not adventure!" she cried.

Janie laughed. "Perhaps adventure is overrated."

Charlotte sat up again. "But you're adventurous," she said. "You go to the lake on your own and dance in the servants' quarters every night and dive off the ha-ha on a dare."

Janie was startled by Charlotte's open admiration of her recklessness.

"That dive earned me a broken collarbone and no pay for the time I took off to heal."

Charlotte was stunned into silence for a moment. But only a moment.

"But you have your mother. She wouldn't let you starve."

"Neither will yours," Janie said, but not with much conviction.

"No, she'll just send me to finishing school." Charlotte's voice was so heavily laden with bitterness, Janie took a step back in shock. "Where I'll learn how to address a letter to a duke and make scintillating conversation with the best of society."

"Those sound like good things," Janie said helplessly. Her sympathy sounded as feeble as it felt.

Charlotte went to the little dressing table in the corner. It had a single mirror that faced the room, reflecting the yellow and green. Charlotte sat down and picked up a hairbrush.

"I don't want to have scintillating conversation. It's meaningless! It's all about roses or church windows or the weather."

"What do you want to talk about?"

Charlotte's eyes met hers in the mirror. "I want to be able to talk like you do, Janie. I want to be able to tease boys and joke with them. Like you do with Harry."

"Harry is like a brother to me," Janie said. "We practically grew up together."

"But you're the same with Lawrence."

*Not entirely*. Janie couldn't tell Charlotte how Lawrence had made her feel like a mouse caught beneath a cobra's gaze. Thrilled and afraid all at once. So she shrugged.

"They're just boys," she said. "Not another species."

Charlotte looked up at Janie with a grin on her face. "Have you met *my* brothers, Janie? Sometimes they seem like they're from a different parentage altogether."

Janie laughed and Charlotte put a hand up over her mouth. "Don't tell *anyone* I said that!"

"Don't worry. Your secret's safe with me."

The door burst open behind her and Charlotte dropped the brush with a clatter on the floor. Janie spun to see Miss

Caldwell framed in the doorway like a model in a fashion magazine, her pink skirts artfully swirled around her ankles. When Miss Caldwell caught sight of Janie, she narrowed her eyes.

Janie picked up the hairbrush and turned away. Charlotte's gaze met hers briefly in the mirror, then slid to the desk under the window.

"You're early," Charlotte said to her friend.

"And hello to you, too," Miss Caldwell sniped. "Your mother sent a message saying you need company. I came to drag you out into the gardens." The Caldwell girl never took her eyes off of Janie.

"I was just . . ." Charlotte stopped. "I was just getting ready to go out."

"Your hair isn't done," the Caldwell girl pointed out.

Charlotte looked helplessly at Janie.

"I was just . . ." Charlotte said again, looking again at the desk. "I'll just be a minute."

Miss Caldwell started picking through the gloves at the top of Charlotte's cedar chest. She looked up and stared pointedly at the brush Janie still clutched to her chest.

"Well, hurry up," she said. "I can't wait all day."

Janie turned and ran the brush experimentally over Charlotte's hair. It slid through the straight, shiny strands like a hand through water. But the Caldwell girl was smart. And observant. She would know Janie wasn't supposed to be there. She obviously remembered that Janie was the kitchen maid.

In the mirror, Janie could see Miss Caldwell trying on a pair of white, opera-length gloves. The girl wrinkled her nose and sniffed at the fingers delicately.

"You need new gloves, Charlotte. These *reek* of cleaning fluid." She stood and pulled at the fingers one by one, gazing down her nose at the book on Charlotte's bedside table.

"I think I'll wear a hat, Janie," Charlotte said loudly. "The blue one. So a simple knot will do."

A knot, Janie could do. She'd done it in her own hair — and her mother's — hundreds of times. She felt her shoulders relax a little. A few more strokes of the hairbrush and a quick twist of the slippery locks.

Miss Caldwell moved around the bed and over toward Charlotte's desk. Janie felt Charlotte stiffen.

"Really, Charlotte," Miss Caldwell said. "All the truly fashionable ladies have their hair put up several times a day." She stared hard at Janie in the mirror. "Even if they're just going out into the garden."

"You seemed in a rush," Charlotte said, slipping a hairpin into Janie's hand like a magician. "And I don't mind. I don't need to dress up for anyone today."

"Oh, yes you do." Miss Caldwell turned to see both of them staring at her in the mirror. "Lord Broadhurst is coming early, too. Didn't your mother tell you?"

Charlotte shook her head wordlessly and Janie went to the wardrobe, hoping the blue hat would be inside.

"On top of the dresser, Janie," Charlotte said quickly, sounding almost breathless. "What do you think, Fran? Mother says it's the latest style."

Charlotte helped Janie set the hat at the correct angle and then held it in place while Janie stuck in the hatpin.

"It's a bit boring," Miss Caldwell said with a critical tilt to her head and turned back to the desk. "What have you been writing, Charlotte? Love letters?"

"It's rubbish." Charlotte stood and swept all the papers into the wastebasket. "Mother wanted me to practice composing menus."

"How jolly dull."

"It's why I'm so glad you're here." Charlotte turned Miss Caldwell away from the desk and squeezed her arm. Janie thought she heard false gaiety in her voice.

"Are you finished?" Miss Caldwell asked, staring again at Janie.

"Thank you, Janie," Charlotte spoke up. No more gaiety. Just cold dismissal.

A spark of wrath fired in Janie's chest until she saw the look of utter hopelessness on Charlotte's face when she glanced once again at her desk. Whatever Charlotte had been writing, it wasn't menus, and she didn't want Miss Caldwell to see it.

"Would you like me to take that, Lady Charlotte?" Janie said, indicating the wastepaper basket.

"That won't be necessary, Janie," Charlotte said, and Miss Caldwell rolled her eyes.

"Sarah will be up soon to tidy your room and collect rubbish for the burner," Janie said, hoping she made her point clear. "If I take it, I could tell her not to bother."

Understanding dawned on Charlotte's face, and for an instant, she looked like she might cry.

"That's very kind, Janie," she said, her voice almost a whisper.

"I'll make sure it gets to the right place," Janie said emphatically, ignoring Miss Caldwell's suspicious gaze.

Janie picked up the basket, narrowly avoiding catching Miss Caldwell's fingers in the wicker. The other girl snatched her hand back and frowned. Janie smiled politely and clasped the basket to her chest, then turned and exited the room.

When she turned down the hall, she nearly ran over Lady Beatrice.

"I'm so sorry," Janie said, juggling the basket and trying to curtsey at the same time. "I didn't see you there."

Lady Beatrice looked her up and down appraisingly. Janie realized she was still wearing the gray cotton dress she wore downstairs. Housemaids at The Manor wore black, with white aprons. Her stomach turned.

"Is Lady Charlotte in her room?" Lady Beatrice asked.

"Yes." Janie bobbed again for good measure. Deference surely counted for something with the rich. "Miss Caldwell is in there with her."

"Oh." Lady Beatrice held very still, looking at the closed door of Charlotte's room. "I see." And she turned away from the door to walk back down the hall to the grand staircase at the end.

Janie watched her for a moment. Lady Beatrice was a puzzling figure. She wore a tight-fitting basque jacket that flared into a peplum at the back. And her skirts were just a trifle too short. The combination — and the jade green color — was all very stylish, but at the same time . . . rebellious.

Before Janie could turn away, Lady Beatrice stopped and spun around.

"Thank you . . ." She paused as one does when waiting to discover someone's name.

"Janie."

"Janie . . ." Lady Beatrice waited. She wanted a last name, as well. How eccentric.

"Janie Seward."

Lady Beatrice smiled, and it changed her face dramatically. She looked even younger. "Thank you, Janie," she said, and walked back toward the stairs.

Janie found the seam of the servants' door and closed it behind her.

The perfect place to hide the papers would be in the cookery book in the kitchen. Janie's mother never opened it — she had all her recipes memorized.

Janie pulled the papers out of the basket. Nothing else lay at the bottom except a desiccated rose and a broken hairpin. Holding the papers in one hand and the basket in the other, she picked her way down the two flights of stairs. The stairwell was narrow with no rail, the risers steep and the runners barely wide enough for a foot. But she was used to running up and down them carrying all sorts of things — including the housemaids' tea — so she wasn't worried about missing a step.

Until she came to the last one and nearly nose-dived into the hall opposite the kitchen. The papers flew from her grasp and the basket twanged, its wicker snapping.

"Blast!" Janie said under her breath. "First the Caldwell girl and now this." She just wasn't cut out for espionage.

A scuffed set of shoes appeared in the doorway in front of her.

"I wondered where you'd gone off to." Harry knelt down and started shuffling up the papers. "Are all of these going out into the burner?"

He lifted one and peered at it.

"No!" Janie cried, and then stopped herself.

"Writing, Janie?" Harry asked, lowering the page and squinting at her. "You're writing?"

"I can, you know," Janie snapped. Better he thought she wrote them than know the truth. If Charlotte was terrified to tell her best friend, Janie should surely keep it a secret from Harry.

"I wasn't saying you're ignorant." Harry studied the top page.

Janie snatched it out of his hand. "It's none of your business."

Harry just looked at her. "No, I guess it's not."

Janie held out her hand for the rest of the papers, and Harry passed them to her silently. He picked up the wastebasket and turned it from side to side. "Where did you get this?"

"From Lady Charlotte. It's broken."

"I can see that." Harry flicked one of the pieces of wicker so it vibrated under his finger and looked at her again. He almost smiled.

Janie felt guilty for lying to him. For being angry with him.

"Thanks," she said, taking it from him.

He nodded his response and walked away.

Janie looked at the page he'd been reading. It was about a dashing Italian count. As far as Janie knew, Charlotte had never met an Italian count. Not even in London when they were there for the Coronation this summer. She hadn't been presented to court yet, and only went to the opera with her mother and once to the Ballets Russes with Lord Andrew Broadhurst.

Janie smiled. Poor Lord Broadhurst. He wasn't going to get very far with Charlotte.

Then Janie stopped smiling. She read along the page, to the description of the man's face. His high cheekbones, his blue eyes — like sapphires. His dark hair, his tall stature.

It was a perfect description of Lawrence. Except for the mouth. Charlotte hadn't gotten the mouth quite right.

Janie thought of the curve of Lawrence's smile and wondered if she was jealous.

Neither one of them could have him. Charlotte couldn't because her mother would have a conniption fit right in the middle of the drawing room. And Janie because even a kiss could get her thrown out of The Manor altogether.

Guiltily, she turned to the next page. It was about the lady mistress of a great house in the country. A kind of a female Bluebeard, who took in helpless maidens and tormented them.

The next page began with a young girl throwing herself into a lake.

The last was about a rich girl with perfect blonde hair and a flair for finding trouble. And making it.

No wonder Charlotte didn't want Miss Caldwell to see what she'd written. The Caldwell girl would probably go straight to Lady Diane. Janie wouldn't put anything past her.

Janie took the cookery book down from the shelf, opened it to the page on custards, and carefully lined up Charlotte's papers so they wouldn't show.

She placed her thoughts of Lawrence and Lady Diane and Miss Caldwell into the book with Charlotte's descriptions of them, and set the entire thing back on the shelf where it belonged.

# Chapter 9

Wasn't that Jenny the kitchen maid?" Fran asked, her voice sounding very loud.

"Janie," Charlotte said. She wondered what Janie would do with her pages. And how she would get them back. Her mother would be apoplectic if she found out Charlotte was writing stories. She equated women writing with Elinor Glyn, with her "shockingly vulgar" romance novels and her not-so-secret affair with Lord Curzon. She assumed every lady writer would end up the same way.

"What was she doing up here?" Fran stood and dropped a bouquet of gloves onto the floor.

Charlotte swooped down on the gloves to hide her panic, dislodging a lock of hair from beneath her hat. Which gave her an idea. And a perfect excuse.

"I'm training her," she said, tucking the hair behind her ear and placing the gloves back in her cedar chest, firmly closing the lid. "To be a lady's maid."

"More like she's training you," Fran sniffed, and marched to the door.

"Maybe it isn't such a bad thing to take a minute to see how the other half lives," Charlotte retorted. She didn't like the look on her friend's face but she crashed on. "Maybe we'll learn to call them by their proper names."

"The other half doesn't matter, Charlotte," Fran said. She cocked her head to one side. "I thought you'd realized that."

Fran opened the door, as Charlotte started to protest. But then Fran stepped back into the room and pushed the door closed behind her, leaning back against it, her eyes wide and alight with mischief.

"Your aunt," Fran whispered. "She's out in the hall."

"What's she doing?" Charlotte asked.

Fran opened the door a crack and peered around it. "Heading for the stairs."

Charlotte strode to the door and reached to pull it open wider, but Fran smacked it shut and turned around.

"I don't want to talk to her. She's odd," Fran said, shrugging and blowing her hair out of her face.

Charlotte bristled. "How do you know? She only arrived yesterday."

"I met her downstairs," Fran said, the words spilling like scattering beads. "She was asking all kinds of questions. About you. About your *cook*. She's nosy."

"Everyone's nosy, Fran, or hadn't you noticed? Gossip is the life's blood of the aristocracy. Without it, the women would have nothing to do."

Fran looked surprised and then laughed. She looped her arm through Charlotte's. "Still, I didn't like that she was asking about you."

"What did you say?"

"That you have never done anything remotely interesting in your life and probably never would."

Charlotte felt like she'd been slapped.

"Why did you say that?"

"To put her off the scent, of course," Fran said reassuringly, though not entirely believably.

When Charlotte reached for the door again, Fran stepped aside, but the hall was empty. Together, the girls walked the length of it, past the Van Dyck. Charlotte remembered Janie's awe, looking at Charles and Henrietta on the wall. Lady Diane loved to remind any and all guests of the Edmonds' family connections to the throne. Extremely distant and tenuous connections. And Charles I was the highlight — which Charlotte herself would care to advertise. The only monarch to be publicly executed by his people? Not something to be proud of.

She suspected it was a copy, but she liked the sentiment. Charles staring lovingly at Henrietta Maria, reaching for her hand, her eyes coyly on the painter.

Charlotte thought about outward appearances. Like the peacock-blue day dress she wore today, with its handmade lace and superior tailoring. Chosen by her mother. Like Charlotte herself, gliding down the stairs arm-in-arm with her best friend, looking the very picture of contentment. The girl of The Manor, who had never done anything interesting and probably never would.

"When do the men arrive?" Fran asked as they crossed the marble hall, her heels clicking on the black and white squares.

"You seem to know more than I do. Didn't you say Lord Broadhurst arrives this afternoon?"

"I meant the other men."

"The 'men' are my father's friends and my brothers." Charlotte supposed she loved her brothers, but all of them had spent her entire life away — first at Eton and then Oxford or Cambridge. She barely knew them.

And when they all came to the house together, Charlotte felt like an afterthought.

"Which ones?" Fran asked as they walked down the short, dark passage to the patio.

"Lord Buckden, Lord Ellis."

"Which *brothers*."

"David, Freddie, and Stephen. John and Edward can't get leave." Lucky devils.

They passed the open door of the gun room, where Harry was polishing the stock of Lord Edmonds's twelve-bore. He looked up at the sound of their voices and Charlotte raised her hand in a little wave, earning a smile.

"That's your hall boy!" Fran said, scandalized. She didn't even try to lower her voice, and Charlotte hustled her out onto the patio before she could say anything offensive.

"That's Harry."

"First the kitchen maid and now this, Charlotte?" Fran asked, sitting down on a patio chair and kicking off her kid-skin shoes. "It's a good thing Lord Broadhurst is coming. You can stop making eyes at the servants."

"Well, I'm not going to start making eyes at Andrew Broadhurst." Charlotte suddenly wanted to run away. From Fran. From The Manor. From expectations.

"Fine," Fran said, putting her stocking feet up on the rail

of the patio. "I'll make eyes at him instead." Charlotte noticed with a twinge of distaste that the soles of Fran's stockings had been stained red by the dye from the shoes.

"Be my guest."

"Don't you think his eyes are like chocolate?" Fran asked. "Sweet and warm, but with a hint of darkness."

"Darkness?" Charlotte perched on the edge of her chair and looked out over the Tudor knot garden, all the hedges arranged in strict lines and bisected by clean gravel pathways. All of them leading nowhere.

"Don't you think?" Fran said, dropping her feet back to the patio stones. "Like he's got secrets. Maybe he's a photographer for the *Daily Mirror*, finding out all the scandal of the upper class and broadcasting it to the world."

Charlotte snorted. "I think you're more of a daydreamer than I am, Fran Caldwell."

"What a horrid sound," Fran said. "You need to stop spending so much time with the servants. And we should both stop daydreaming and set all of our minds' energy on catching husbands."

"Oh, Fran, have *you* been spending too much time with my mother?"

"It's true, though," Fran said. "If we start catching the eyes of eligible men now, we will surely have three or four proposals *each* by August next year. Just in time for the Season."

"Is that all you ever think of?"

"It should be all *you* ever think of, Charlotte. Think of the freedom! You'll be able to make your own menus and pay your own calls. Choose your own charities."

Charlotte felt her face flush. "Freedom? It's just another prison! There's more to life than choosing between turbot or salmon!"

"Not our lives, Charlotte," Fran said, thrusting her feet back into her slippers. "The sooner you realize that, the better. Or you may discover that you've lost that charmingly rich young man who is coming to The Manor expressly to see *you*."

"Charming?" Charlotte asked. Her palms had begun to itch. If she didn't get away from Fran soon, she might tell her what she really thought.

"Lord Broadhurst is a catch, no doubt about it. I don't know what's the matter with you lately. I have no idea what you're thinking, but your mind obviously isn't in the game. It's like you don't even care who you marry!"

Charlotte stood and turned on her friend.

"I *don't* care who I marry right now, Fran! I'm only sixteen years old! There are things I want to do, a life I want to live and adventures to have before I end up shackled to some dull earl-in-waiting whose greatest joy in life is bloody cricket!"

Silence bloomed between them. Charlotte returned Fran's glare without flinching. She couldn't believe she had once thought Fran daring and gregarious and someone to be envied.

By the same token she couldn't believe she had just said all of that out loud.

Before she could open her mouth to apologize, a strangled sound like a cross between a cleared throat and a bark caused them both to spin toward The Manor.

And there, where the doors had been opened to let the summer air into the house, stood Andrew Broadhurst, dressed in a crisp, well-tailored linen suit, his cobalt cravat bringing out the darkness in his eyes.

"Lord Broadhurst." Fran curtseyed and then smirked at Charlotte. "How lovely that you are already here."

"I came early to see the . . ." Andrew cleared his throat again. ". . . the village cricket team."

Charlotte wanted to sink right down through the sandstone paving.

"Welcome to The Manor," she said. Wishing she were anywhere else. Wishing for rescue from her own imprudent remarks.

She spied Lawrence stepping onto the terrace behind Andrew and her expression cracked into a true smile.

"Would you join us for tea?" she asked — barely glancing at Andrew or waiting for his assent while passing him to get to Lawrence.

"Save me!" she whispered.

"Dear Princess, I'd save you from the fiercest dragon," Lawrence said with a quick bow, then glanced over her head. "But I'm not sure there's anything I can do to save you from boredom. Or Miss Caldwell."

Charlotte tried not to giggle.

"Perhaps just tea, then," she said. "And cakes. Please, Lawrence." She stopped herself from reaching out for his arm. "I think I'll need cakes."

"Your wish is my command."

Charlotte lingered, watching his retreat and enjoying how the back of his tailcoat nipped in at the waist. She imagined the two of them together on a luxury liner to a new life in America, where class and status and family alliances didn't matter.

Charlotte turned and almost ran into Fran, who had crept up silently behind her. Fran had a shrewd look on her face, and a calculating half smile.

"I said he was handsome before, didn't I?" Fran asked, nodding to the far door where Lawrence had disappeared. "Things you want to do, eh?" she asked quietly. "And I thought you meant adventures like Nellie Bly or Mary Kingsley — discovering new lands and traveling to undiscovered places."

Before Charlotte could defend herself, Fran turned back to the patio and walked over to Andrew Broadhurst, resting her gloved hand briefly on his arm, the skirt of her tea gown swirling around her ankles like a wave. Andrew nodded at something Fran said, and then looked up to smile at Charlotte, who was surprised by the humor in those dark eyes. As if he knew something she didn't. Or as if they shared a secret joke.

Her throat suddenly felt dry. "I've just ordered tea."

"As if anyone would want a hot drink on an afternoon like this." Fran threw herself back into her chair, one hand dramatically on her forehead.

"I can request barley water as well." Irritation rose up in Charlotte again. And the itchiness to escape.

Fran rolled her eyes. "Did you at least order cakes?"

"Of course." Charlotte managed to keep her voice level.

"Chocolate?" Fran tipped her head coyly at Lord Broadhurst. "They're my favorite."

"I didn't specify." It was incredibly difficult to speak through gritted teeth.

"Well, by all means, please specify," Fran said, snagging Charlotte's hand and reeling her in like a fish. She leaned in, as if to whisper another request, her words grazing Charlotte's ear.

"You're not doing yourself any favors, Charlotte. Mark my words. You have to reach out and grab life, or it will pass you by."

"Is that why you're here?" Charlotte hissed in reply. "To grab my brother?"

Fran's gaze didn't flicker. "Clever girl."

Charlotte stormed back into the house, the dim light a blinding contrast to the oppressive sunshine outside.

"Fran and her manipulation," she grumbled out loud. "Why can't men see right through her? I should warn David." Charlotte shuddered involuntarily, thinking of Fran as her sister-in-law. As mistress of The Manor.

She stopped in the middle of the marble hall. Fran was her best friend. Charlotte shook her head. But right now, she almost hated her.

Charlotte grabbed the bell pull, but dropped it again without yanking it. Fran might be an irritant, but like it or not, she was right. Charlotte had to seize life while she could. She had to go for what she wanted.

With that thought, a series of images flashed across her mind. Not imaginings, but rememberings. Like a moving picture at the cinema. Lawrence helping her away from the lake. Daring her to eat a chili. Dancing the hesitation waltz.

Charlotte didn't want the possibility of more to pass her by.

Charlotte looked back toward the patio, but could no longer see Fran and Andrew. So she turned away from the bell pull and ran across the checkerboard floor, not even glancing into the gun room. Hoping that Harry didn't see her, because, like the other servants, he was under orders to keep her upstairs.

She hadn't used the hidden door behind the staircase since her childhood, but she remembered it was there. David had walked her through it more than once. At the age of five, it seemed a doorway into a magical place — like Alice's rabbit hole. She opened it, catching the odors of coal fires and roast, cabbage and cleaning fluid. A short flight of stairs disappeared into the basement.

"The only way forward is down, I suppose," Charlotte said to herself, and closed the door behind her.

A crash and a clatter down the hall were followed by a sharp cry — pain? Anger? Frustration? It must have come from the kitchen.

Charlotte held her breath. What if someone caught her down here? Foyle, the formidable butler, of whom Charlotte had always been a little afraid as a little girl. Or Mrs. Griffiths.

Her mother would send her immediately to finishing school. Shooting party or not.

*I'm not cut out for this,* Charlotte thought. *I could never be a lady spy like Belle Boyd.*

Charlotte took three steps backward, up the stairs. Just in time to see feet come out into the hall in front of her — from the plain white door on the left.

The men's quarters.

Charlotte flattened herself against the wall, watching the shoes and hoping whoever it was wouldn't look her way. Only when he walked off did she recognize the shape of his back. She watched until he turned through a doorway. The footman's closet, where they hung their livery jackets.

Charlotte imagined she was someone strong, someone courageous. Someone worth loving. She straightened her shoulders and walked down the corridor, looking neither right nor left.

Straight ahead, she saw a skirt flash by the door of the kitchen. Mrs. Seward's gray dress. Another clatter. Charlotte paused, ready to run, but heard the murmur of voices rise up again.

The thought that Lawrence might be in there flirting with one of the maids briefly flashed in her mind, but she nudged it out of the way.

Charlotte turned and slipped into the footman's closet. The room was tiny and smelled of shoe black and soap. Of lemons.

"Lady Charlotte! What are you doing here?"

Charlotte nearly fainted from relief.

"Lawrence!"

She grabbed his hand and pulled the door closed behind her, leaving just enough of a gap to let her see his face. His eyebrows arched in surprise, his eyes unsure, and his mouth tipped into a smile.

He was happy to see her.

All she could think about was Lawrence's hand in hers. About the possibility that he might one day kiss a different girl. And the fact that she had to take her chances when they arose.

Charlotte's sudden bravery overtook her and she stood on her tiptoes and wrapped her arms around his neck. She felt him pull back — just a little, and just for a moment — and then he moved forward and pressed her gently against the wall.

Charlotte's heart slammed against her rib cage as she tilted up her face to meet his kiss.

# Chapter 10

Janie always felt life slow down when she was doing something methodical. Reducing soups, kneading bread, icing cakes. She couldn't rush or worry. She could only do.

"Cakes!" Lawrence crowed, coming into the kitchen. He straightened his jacket and used his thumb to wipe the corner of his mouth.

Janie indicated the kitchen table — the bowls of icing covered with damp cloths and the fingers of sponge she'd been cutting exactly two inches long by a half inch wide.

"Perfect." Lawrence sneaked a finger of sponge off the table and ducked away from Janie when she tried to swat him.

"You're far too cheerful to be believed," she teased.

"What's not to be cheerful about?" Lawrence spun her once around and turned back to the table. "How long does it take to ice these? Lady Charlotte asked for cakes explicitly. She's having tea with Miss Caldwell and Lord Broadhurst."

Janie snorted. "Lord *Andrew* Broadhurst? The earl's son? That's not going to make her happy."

Lawrence stopped, another scrap of cake halfway to his mouth.

"She doesn't like him?" he asked.

Janie narrowed her eyes. "I don't think he's poetic enough for her. He's one of those classic English lords, with more marble than good sense. He loves cricket and polo and the weather, whereas she loves poetry and adventure."

Lawrence laughed. "Hardly a match made in heaven, then?"

"The drawing room, more like. She's a rich and hopeless romantic, Lawrence," Janie said seriously as she deftly smoothed pink royal icing over a finger of cake and laid it on a tray. "A dangerous combination."

"Hopeless?"

"Rich."

Lawrence nodded. "I shall bear this in mind."

"I'll just finish these, and there is some fruitcake for slicing, too."

"Miss Caldwell wants chocolate."

"Well, Miss Caldwell will just have to sing for it."

Janie tried to suppress the feeling of glee at thwarting the crafty girl.

"And tea?" Lawrence said, carefully arranging slices of fruitcake on a silver dish.

"The kettle has just boiled, but the china is still in the servery."

Lawrence brought the teapot and Janie spooned in the leaves; then he held the pot while she poured the just-boiled water into it. A good kitchen — a good household — ran like clockwork, as clichéd as that might sound. All the cogs running together, never missing a beat, the mechanism smooth and untroubled, with no grit or extra grease to make it scratch or slip.

Just the way it should be.

"Thanks, Janie," Lawrence said. He slipped his gloves back on, hefted the tray onto his left shoulder, and leaned over to kiss her on the forehead. "You're a star."

Janie felt the mechanism fail, catching on a fine piece of trouble in the gears. She watched Lawrence go.

Then she turned and reached down the cookbook from the shelf, opening it to Charlotte's pages. She flattened them open and reread the description of the Italian count. She didn't know if she was jealous or afraid, or a little of both.

"I should just get on with my job and be neither," she said to herself, pressing the book closed. As she replaced it on the shelf and turned back to the icing, she thought she saw a flutter of pink at the window.

"My brain's gone pink," she muttered.

Then a flutter of jade green at the door made her look up and catch sight of Lady Beatrice.

"Oh!" Janie said, dropping the finger of sponge and its still-sticky icing. Pink splotched on the toe of her shoe.

"I *am* sorry," Lady Beatrice said, stepping into the kitchen. "I didn't mean to startle you." Her voice was so different from Lady Diane's. It was deeper, a rich contralto, and her inflections were different — probably affected by her years abroad. Her honey blonde hair trailed unruly wisps around features softer than her sister's.

"It's all right," Janie said and waved a hand at the table. "There's plenty more where that came from."

She was very glad Lady Beatrice hadn't come in a few minutes earlier and seen Charlotte's writing. Or worse, seen Lawrence's affectionate peck on her forehead. It could so easily be misconstrued.

Janie wondered if she herself had misunderstood it.

"I can see that," Lady Beatrice said. There was a smile in her voice. Something one rarely heard in Lady Diane's.

"Can I get you something? Lawrence just took tea up to Lady Charlotte on the patio."

Lady Beatrice looked out the kitchen door as if she could see the group on the patio through the walls.

"Actually," she said, "I was hoping to speak with the cook, Mrs. Seward."

Cold dread settled low in Janie's belly. "She's having her tea."

Lady Beatrice stepped farther into the room and rested her fingertips on the scarred tabletop. Long, thin fingers. An ink stain on the index finger of her right hand.

"You said your name was Seward, didn't you, Janie?" she asked.

"Yes, ma'am. I'm the cook's daughter."

Lady Beatrice looked at her as if trying to see behind her words. Then she arranged another smile on her face. "To the manor born."

"I was born here, yes," Janie said. "But my father joined the Army soon after, and we moved."

"But you came back."

"My father died. In Africa."

"I heard."

Janie looked up from the cake she was icing. "You knew him?"

"I lived here after my own father died. My sister was kind enough to take me in until I — until I married. I remember your mother's cooking fondly. I have yet to find someone who can make a roast or cook a vanilla soufflé as well as she can."

Janie thought she might cry. Lady Beatrice loved her mother's cooking. Lady Beatrice was going to offer her mother swags of money to move out to Italy or some other distant place. A place where a single woman living alone would need a cook.

But not a kitchen maid.

"You're a cook yourself, I see."

"Just the second kitchen maid."

"Well, if your mother is training you, I'm sure your skills already rival some of the other houses in the neighborhood. Those cakes look delicious."

Janie kept her eyes on the cakes so Lady Beatrice wouldn't see her aggrieved expression. She hated to be patronized. Especially by someone about to rip her life apart.

"May I?" Lady Beatrice's long fingers extended to the already-frosted cakes.

Janie nodded, her hand gripping the edge of the table.

Lady Beatrice delicately picked up a piece of cake and nibbled the end. She closed her eyes.

"Delicious," she said and then opened them again. Hazel eyes. Not blue, like Lady Diane's. "You'll go far, Janie Seward."

"I'm happy to be here for now," Janie said, and pulled the bowl of frosting closer. "With my mother."

"Of course you are," Lady Beatrice said, and then lowered her voice, almost as if speaking to herself. "A girl should be with her mother."

A new knot of anxiety bubbled in Janie's throat. What if Lady Beatrice asked *both* of them? What would she choose — her mother? Or her home?

"Why were you upstairs?" Lady Beatrice asked.

Cold dread hardened below Janie's breastbone. The woman in front of her had every tool needed to ruin her life. She could take her mother away. She could tell Lady Diane about her secret wanderings around the house.

"Lady Charlotte asked me."

"Why?" Lady Beatrice reached casually for another cake, and Janie let silence settle as she scraped the bottom of the bowl of icing as if the answer to the question lay there.

"No chocolate?"

Miss Caldwell stood in the door, one hand on each side of the frame. She glared at Janie, but Janie felt she'd never been so glad to see the Caldwell girl in her life.

"I'm sorry, Miss Caldwell," Janie said hurriedly. "Lady Diane ordered yellow sponge. I can make sure we have chocolate for tomorrow."

"Tomorrow?" the girl asked. Her voice was low and growly. More dangerous than it would have been as a shriek.

"Thank you for the cake, Janie," Lady Beatrice said, moving toward the door. "And the chat." She paused and spoke directly to Miss Caldwell. "We should let Janie get on with her work."

"I just have one more request, Lady Beatrice," the Caldwell girl said airily. "Won't be a moment." She paused, waiting for Lady Beatrice to pass her by. "I'll see you at dinner."

Lady Beatrice flashed an indecipherable look at the girl, and then left the kitchen. Janie noticed she turned left — toward the servants' staircase — instead of right to exit through the courtyard.

Miss Caldwell watched her go and then stalked into the kitchen.

"You could show a little deference," Miss Caldwell said. "Or don't you think the rules apply to you?"

"I try my best, Miss Caldwell." Janie laced her words with submissiveness but seethed inside.

"Well, you'll have to try better than that," Miss Caldwell hissed, looking ready to strike. "A *good* servant turns away from her betters when seeing them in the hall. A *good* servant is invisible. She doesn't wear filthy kitchen clothes upstairs."

Miss Caldwell flicked a hand toward Janie's limp cap and stained apron.

"A good servant knows her place. She knows what's wanted before anyone else. You should have had chocolate. Just in case."

Janie stared at her silently.

"A good servant . . ." Miss Caldwell was right up in Janie's face. ". . . does not raise her eyes to her mistress."

Janie knew she should look down at her feet. At her hands clasped before her. She knew she should bow her head.

But she didn't. Instead she looked Miss Caldwell directly in the eye.

"You are not my mistress."

Miss Caldwell's face drained of all color, and Janie felt a swell of triumph.

"If you'll excuse me, Miss Caldwell," Janie said, again lacing her tone with deference, "I have work to do."

She turned and walked away into the larder, where she could catch her breath and calm her heart in the cool, blank darkness.

*I* think I'll wear red tonight." Fran lounged on Charlotte's bed, her voice setting Charlotte's teeth on edge. "David likes red, doesn't he?"

"I haven't the faintest." Charlotte wished Fran would go away. She wanted to write. She wanted to put a scene in her story where the Italian count kissed the heroine.

"He's your *brother*," Fran said. "You have to know."

"He's twelve years older than I am."

"And still not married," Fran mused.

Charlotte tuned her out as she went on about bugle beads and handkerchief hems.

The only thing Charlotte could think of was Lawrence's lips on hers. Surprisingly soft, and tasting of raspberry jam.

Charlotte licked her lips. Or perhaps raspberry coulis.

Charlotte smiled. Raspberry coulis was part of her mother's dinner menu. She knew Lawrence's secret now. That he tasted the food from the kitchen. Perhaps when no one was looking.

"And my dress isn't really red, I suppose," Fran said. "More of a raspberry color."

"I love raspberries," Charlotte said, and giggled, feeling like an infatuated girl in a penny romance.

"You really are wretchedly poor company today, Charlotte." Fran blew her hair out of her face and stood. "Maybe if I leave you alone, you'll be more sensible at dinner."

Charlotte tried to arrange her face into an appropriately contrite expression. She might have twenty minutes to write.

"Why would your aunt be talking to that Janie person?" Fran's question cut across Charlotte's distraction. Her eyes narrowed when Charlotte looked up sharply. "And why on earth would she be in the kitchen?"

"Why were you?" Charlotte retorted, but she was thinking about what Janie may have discovered.

"I went to see where they had hidden the chocolate cakes."

"Mrs. Seward doesn't hide cakes."

"How do you know? Servants could be stealing things right out from under your nose and you'd be too busy daydreaming to notice."

There was a knock at the door, and Sarah the housemaid entered. "I've come to see if there's anything you need before we have our dinner, Lady Charlotte."

"Why didn't Janie come up?" Fran asked, her eyes wide with counterfeit innocence. "Since she's being trained as a lady's maid."

Sarah's face registered surprise, injury, and anger, and then went blank, all in the space of a few seconds.

"Janie?" She looked at Charlotte for confirmation.

Charlotte tried to shrug casually. "She's a smart girl. She could be better than a cook. Send her up, Sarah."

Sarah nodded mutely, and Fran flounced out of the room after her. Charlotte finally felt able to breathe. She lay back on her bed, looking up at the canopy, letting her mind drift. She didn't need to daydream about possibilities anymore. She could daydream about reality.

A swift knock on the door interrupted her thoughts and Sarah entered, looking mightily cross. She curtseyed quickly, not looking Charlotte in the eye.

"Janie, my lady," she said.

Janie came into the room looking at least as cross as Sarah.

She had flour on her apron, and her cap was limp from the steam of the kitchen.

"Janie!" Charlotte said and stood up, but Sarah hadn't moved.

"That will be all, Sarah."

Sarah paused. A tiny hesitation, as if she was considering talking back. But she just curtseyed again, threw a furious glance at Janie, and shut the door behind her.

"I thought we were keeping this a secret," Janie said before Charlotte could speak.

"We —" Charlotte stuttered. "We are."

"Miss Caldwell knows," Janie said. "Sarah knows."

"I told them I'm training you to be a lady's maid."

"But you're not." Janie's face was like granite.

"I could," Charlotte said, warming to the idea. "I'd rescue you from drudgery and dishes."

"I don't want to be rescued." Janie wouldn't even look at her. Why was she so recalcitrant? She was like a mule. Resistant to change. Resistant to everything.

"What's the matter?"

"What's the matter?" Janie finally looked up. "I just left a kitchen full of unpeeled potatoes to come up here. I *have* a job. I don't do hair. I don't know a diamond from paste. I'm not fit to be a lady's maid."

Charlotte stood and wrapped Janie in a hug, but dropped her arms immediately when the other girl flinched.

"Of course you're good enough to be a lady's maid, Janie. You're bright and . . . and . . . and eloquent. You shouldn't run yourself down so."

"I am content with my station in life." Janie's voice was as brittle as the stiffness in her limbs.

Charlotte recognized one of her mother's personal vexations. Lady Diane complained about servants who left The Manor to work in the city. About scullery maids who wanted to go to the local school. About the working poor who emigrated to America. About Charlotte wanting more than marriage and menus and calling cards. Lady Diane said everyone should be content with his or her station in life. As she was.

"Well, you shouldn't be."

Janie looked like she'd been slapped, but didn't lift her gaze from her hands clasped in front of her. "You know best, Lady Charlotte."

The silence that followed rang tinny and loud in Charlotte's ears, and she felt the afternoon's cakes thick and sweet in the back of her throat.

"Don't you want to be more?" Charlotte asked. "My mother wants me to marry Andrew Broadhurst. To be a countess. But I want to wait for someone better for *me*. Don't you see? I want to be with someone I can . . . enjoy kissing. Someone who can hold a conversation about something that interests *me*. I don't just want to be a wife. I want to be a . . . a . . . *person*. Don't you?"

"I only ever wanted to be a cook," Janie said, the defiance returning to her voice. "It's what I'm good at."

"But what about love?" Charlotte asked. She almost asked about Harry. She could imagine Janie and Harry together. Easily.

Janie looked up at her. "It earned my mother nothing but heartbreak. And it made her lose her job."

"Why are there all these rules?" Charlotte cried.

Janie looked startled. "It's the way things are," she said, and her tone was so matter-of-fact that Charlotte almost believed her. "Though maybe not the way we'd like them to be."

*Almost* believed her.

"I have to think things can be different," Charlotte said vehemently. "That things can change. Or my life will be over when Lord Broadhurst finally proposes."

Charlotte was surprised when Janie laughed.

"It's probably not necessary to be so dramatic," Janie said. "But let's see what we can do to stem the tide of the apocalypse, shall we?"

Charlotte laughed, too.

"Let's give a little truth to our lie, as well," she said, and pushed Janie toward the dressing table. "Sit."

"What are you going to do?" Janie looked up over her shoulder.

"Show you how to do a chignon." Charlotte turned Janie's face toward the mirror and loosened her hair. It fell in thick waves, a deep rich brown with those red highlights.

"Oh, Janie, you have such lovely hair," Charlotte said, picking it up and hefting the weight of it.

Janie just pursed her lips together, but Charlotte noticed she looked pleased.

Charlotte reached for her hairbrush and began running it through Janie's hair in long, deft strokes. Janie winced once or twice when it caught in a tangle, but then closed her eyes and leaned back in the chair, letting Charlotte's hands run through the long strands.

"Your aunt was downstairs," Janie said. "She was asking about my mother."

Charlotte paused. Aunt Beatrice got more intriguing by the hour.

"Why?"

Janie sighed. "I think she's offered her a job."

"Oh." Charlotte twisted the hair into a rope, smoothing strands as she went. She wondered if Mrs. Seward would take the job. If she'd take Janie with her. But Charlotte had just found Janie. She couldn't stand to see her go. She wondered if she could convince her mother to keep Janie on as a maid. "Watch."

Janie's eyes opened. "Don't tell Lady Diane," she said. "Please. Just *thinking* of going somewhere else could get Ma sacked."

Charlotte nodded and curled the rope around itself, tucking the end beneath the rest, making sure all the pieces that might frizz were well hidden.

"Would you go, too?" she asked, trying to sound casual.

"Lady Beatrice is only one person." Janie's voice sounded small and scared. "I don't think she'll need a kitchen maid."

Relief tingled all the way down to Charlotte's fingers. Until she realized they were the only things holding Janie's hair up.

"Oh, blast."

Janie's shocked gaze met hers in the mirror.

"I forgot that I need pins," Charlotte explained. "Sarah always has a handful tucked into her apron pocket. Can you reach them? In that little cloisonné chest."

They moved together so Janie could reach the far end of the dressing table. She unclasped the lid and revealed a porcupine of hairpins and hatpins, a broken earring, and a button. She handed Charlotte three hairpins and pulled out the button.

"This isn't one of yours."

Janie was right. Charlotte had found the plain bone button on the street in London. She liked the feel of it. Worn and smooth. She liked to wonder who had lost it. To imagine the places the button had been.

"I found it and couldn't throw it away." Charlotte slid a hairpin beneath the knot, securing it.

"Why don't you put it in your button box?"

Charlotte felt a blush starting to rise. "I don't have one."

Janie turned, nearly wrenching the almost-complete knot out of Charlotte's hands. She stopped dead still and waited for Charlotte to push in the last pin. Then she turned all the way around and looked Charlotte full in the face.

"You don't have a button box? A sewing basket?"

"I have my tapestry basket. And embroidery floss."

"Of course. You wouldn't need to mend your stockings or replace a button."

Charlotte thought she heard a tinge of derision in Janie's tone. She looked down at her hands. So useless most of the time. Useless for anything but writing letters or holding a calling card, or occasionally the reins of a well-trained horse.

When she looked up again, she expected to see a pitying look on Janie's face. Instead, she saw a look of wonder. Janie's hand was up, touching the nape of her neck, stroking upward from her ears.

"How did you do that?" she asked.

Charlotte saw a slim girl in a gray cotton dress. A long neck exposed by the absence of hair. The simple, elegant knot changed the shape of Janie's face. Made her cheekbones more prominent. The shape of her eyes more visible. More green than hazel, and quite extraordinary.

"You're beautiful," Charlotte said.

Janie stood. "Don't be daft." But her eyes flicked back to her own reflection.

Charlotte smiled and sat down. "Your turn."

Janie stepped back and shook her head. "I can't."

Charlotte unpinned her own hair and held out the brush. "I tell you what, I'll teach you how to do a chignon if you teach me how to sew on a button."

"I can teach you how to make toast, as well."

Charlotte laughed and relaxed into the feel of Janie's hands in her hair. She'd read stories about girls who brushed each other's hair. It made them seem like best friends. As she guided Janie through the steps, she imagined them pretending to be sisters, living out of suitcases, having adventures. Seeing the frescoes of Florence and exploring the Colosseum in Rome. Or heading off to Antarctica like the Scott expedition. Or to America on the boat they were building in Belfast — one of the biggest ships in the world.

Janie stuck the tip of her tongue just out of the corner of her mouth while setting the hairpins. Charlotte grinned, remembering how she did the same when learning to play the piano. Until her mother shamed her out of the habit.

"What do you think?" Janie whispered.

Loose strands of hair floated around the lopsided knot like a halo.

"I think it's perfect." Charlotte saw the disbelief register on Janie's face and amended. "For a first attempt."

The corner of Janie's mouth curved upward. "Are you suggesting there's going to be another?"

"I need an excuse to get you up here," Charlotte said, standing up. "I don't have anyone else to talk to." She realized she sounded pathetic, so she put on a bright smile. "And how else am I going to find out all your secrets?"

Janie darted a glance at her and rubbed the back of her neck. "I don't really have any secrets."

"I mean about Aunt Beatrice," Charlotte said hurriedly.

She hadn't meant to be nosy. After all, she didn't want to tell anyone her secrets, either. The only way she could tell was to make them into a story.

"Janie!" she said, remembering. "Thank you for saving my writing from Fran earlier. She . . . she never would have understood."

"I'll get the pages back to you."

"I know." Charlotte bit her lip. "I'm glad you're my friend."

"I'm your servant, Lady Charlotte," Janie said sadly. "And neither one of us should forget it."

# Chapter 12

"Fancy the skivvy becoming a lady's maid."

Lawrence caught Janie on the back stairs before she made it to the basement.

Irritation flashed through her. "I'm not a skivvy."

"I didn't mean any harm by it, Janie," Lawrence said. He leaned back against the wall and looked at her with those hooded blue eyes. "I think it's a good thing to try to better yourself."

"I'm not going to be a lady's maid. I want to be a cook." She thought about telling him how gratifying it was to transform butter and flour and stock into *sauce velouté.* But she didn't think he'd understand. "So I think I'll just remain a kitchen maid."

"You want to spend your life icing thousands of fingers of cakes? And slopping out the pig bucket?"

"I'm willing to put in the work so I can end up doing the thing I love."

Lawrence studied her as one might an unknown species and Janie squirmed a little under his scrutiny.

"You really love what you do?"

Janie almost laughed. "I do. I like feeding people."

"I wish there was something I loved that much."

Janie looked up into Lawrence's face. He was the perfect vision of a footman — tall and handsome. Pleasant to look at and gentle in his service. His blue eyes bright and warm . . .

She wasn't sure how long they stood there before Lawrence reached up his right hand to tuck a stray hair behind her ear.

"You're beautiful, you know that?" he said. Just as Charlotte had — but it sounded very different coming from Lawrence.

His fingers remained on her temple, sending little flares of sensation across her skin and down her throat. She wanted to believe him. She wanted to be beautiful.

She wanted to rest her cheek in the palm of his hand and hear him say it again.

As if he could hear her thoughts, his lips curved into a smile and his gaze moved from her eyes to her mouth.

He was going to kiss her. She had never been kissed before, but she knew. Sure as she knew her own name.

"I —" Janie put a hand on his chest, panic and exhilaration pinching her ribs and lifting her onto her toes.

A single kiss could cost her her job. Her career. Her life.

"Can't."

Janie dropped back to her heels and stepped away. It was like coming out of a dream. Out of a spell. Reality came back in a rush — the clatter of pans in the kitchen, laughter from the servants' hall, the soft thunk of the door above them closing. Without looking back at Lawrence, she made her way down the last five steps to the basement.

Mrs. Seward had the night off, so the kitchen maids were in charge of the meal for the family and their two unexpected guests. Just a "simple supper" — only five courses. All the prep work had been done earlier in the day, and the cold meat was ready for the servants' supper, so Janie set a kettle on the stove and sat wearily in a chair at the kitchen table. And tried to digest what had just happened.

Tess, the head kitchen maid, wheeled on her. She had a spoon in each hand, and sweat beaded on her forehead.

"Well, look at you, Miss High-and-Mighty. Too big to make your own tea now? Don't think you can get away with that here with your mother gone. We need all the help we can get. Right, Mollie?"

Tess looked over Janie's head and when Janie turned, she saw Mollie nodding, her eyes hard and bitter.

Janie refused to rise for the bait. "I am perfectly capable of making my own tea."

"You're certainly right you are," Tess said triumphantly. "And you're not too good to make the servants' dinner, either. Or scrub the floor."

"I've done that every day for the past four years, Tess McKinnon. I'm unlikely to stop now, you know."

"Sarah says you're training to be a lady's maid," Tess ranted. "I know what you upstairs maids are like. They're too good for the likes of us. Skivvies, we are, Mollie."

"Don't drag her into this," Janie said, her ire finally pushing her to her feet.

"Don't think you can tell me what to do, either, *Janie*. You work for me here."

Janie took a step back. She and Tess had always worked well together. They didn't share secrets or go to the pictures, but they got along. They got the work done.

"I refuse to call you 'Miss Seward,' I refuse to show you deference, and I refuse to wait on you. I'd rather lick my pots than yours any day."

"What's that supposed to mean?" Janie asked.

Tess just turned her back. But Mollie laughed from the scullery doorway.

"It means," Mollie said in her high, clear voice, "that the upstairs maids clean the chamber pots. We would never get our hands so mucky."

Janie stared as Mollie went back to the sink full of dishes. She didn't even want to be a lady's maid. It wasn't even real.

When the dressing gong sounded, Janie went in to clear away the dinner dishes in the servants' hall, getting caught in the hurricane as the servants rushed to down a final gulp of tea or the last piece of meat on the plate. Bells rang in the hall — Lady Diane's, Miss Caldwell's, Lord Edmonds's.

"The potatoes were cold," Sarah told Janie coolly. "Just because you have a fancy hairstyle doesn't mean you can get away without feeding us."

"I did feed you," Janie snapped. She had forgotten about her hair. Or, to be honest, she'd left it because it made her feel pretty. Prettier than she'd ever been in the drab gray dress splattered with gravy and soaked in greasy water.

"I couldn't eat them." Sarah pushed her plate away and left the room.

What she'd left behind was equal to what would have been served to Janie and her two girl cousins on Romney Marsh. Sometimes, that was all they got, because the men got the bacon or the bit of mutton. When it was available.

"Defeated by a plate of potatoes," she said quietly, and picked it up and tipped it over the slop bucket. It made her want to cry. And she hated crying.

"Don't let her get to you," Harry said. Janie had forgotten that he still sat at the table. "She's just jealous."

"Of me?"

"Of your promotion." Harry put a ribbon into his book and set it down on the table.

"Hardly a promotion," Janie snorted. "And it's meant to be a secret."

"Not much of a secret anymore."

Janie stopped and stood very still, refusing to blink or look at him until the threatening tears subsided.

"It's one of the Ten Commandments. 'Thou shalt not better yourself.' "

Janie sniffed. "I'm not trying to." She tossed the last remnants of the servants' supper into the pig bucket. So much waste. Her outrage at the inequity seared her from the inside. "I'm fit only to gather scraps and scrub the floors."

"That's not what I meant." Harry's unruffled — almost teasing — defense only infuriated her more, and she considered throwing the bucket and its contents at him. But she knew the only person who would clean it up was her. So she dropped the bucket instead and turned to leave the room.

"Where are you going?" Harry reached for her, but Janie jerked out of his grasp.

"I'm going back to my place, Harry Peasgood, in the *kitchen*. Why don't you skulk off to the soot and coal scuttles? Where *you* belong."

Swallowing her guilt along with the unshed tears, Janie went back to the kitchen. It felt more like a sauna than usual, the rising temperature outside outmatched by the temperature inside.

Janie gathered a little pile of mushrooms for the *sauce aux champignons* and attacked them with the French knife, hacking them into smaller and smaller pieces.

"Rather be doing your swanky work?" Mollie goaded. "No need to take it out on the mushrooms."

Janie felt the last remnants of her restraint leave her and she slapped the knife down on the table. "I'll take it out on you if you like."

"That's quite enough of that, young lady." A new voice came from behind her.

Janie turned. Mrs. Griffiths, the housekeeper, stood in the doorway, keys jangling from her waist. Out of the corner of her eye, Janie saw Mollie smirk.

"I think it's time we had a little chat, Janie," the housekeeper said. "Please see me in my sitting room."

"Those mushrooms aren't going to chop themselves," Tess muttered when Mrs. Griffiths was out of earshot.

"I'm coming back," Janie said.

Tess may have smiled. "I wouldn't bet on it."

Janie wiped her hands on her apron, noticed the stains already on it, and took it off, laying it on the table next to the mushrooms. Hoping she would come back.

"Close the door," Mrs. Griffiths said when Janie came into her little sitting room. A plate of Janie's cakes sat on the desk, a single china cup next to it. The room smelled of lavender and tea, furniture polish, and regulations.

Mrs. Griffiths didn't invite her to sit. Janie kept her eyes on the edge of the desk, not looking into the housekeeper's face. Showing deference.

"Look at me, Janie."

Mrs. Griffiths had a penetrating gaze, the kind you'd expect from a school matron. Or a government interrogator.

Brawling was explicitly prohibited among the servants. But Janie would never have hit Mollie. Surely Mrs. Griffiths knew that.

"Some disturbing news has come to my attention."

Janie blinked. "This isn't about what I said to Mollie?"

"It is and it isn't."

Mrs. Griffiths reached into the desk drawer in front of her and extracted a sheaf of papers, folded neatly in the middle. Janie couldn't stifle her gasp.

"Did you put these in the cookery book in the kitchen, Janie?"

"Yes." Janie hung her head again. "I did."

Poor Charlotte. Janie wanted to curse her and her half-baked secrets, and wanted to curse herself for not hiding them better. Shame tingled at the backs of her knees and the base of her skull.

"Is this part of your campaign to better yourself?"

Janie looked up quizzically. "I'm not sure what you mean, Mrs. Griffiths."

"When do you find time to write, Janie?" Mrs. Griffiths said. "Are you neglecting your work?"

"No!" Janie cried.

"Don't use that tone with me, young lady." Mrs. Griffiths stood. "You're in the wrong here, and you know it. We have nothing against writing *per se*, but it does seem to indicate that you have too much time on your hands. Are you telling us that your position isn't necessary?"

"No, Mrs. Griffiths," Janie said hastily. "I'm not telling you anything."

"Oh." The housekeeper closed her mouth with a snap like the metal clasp of a purse.

"I mean, that isn't what I meant to say. Mother — Mrs. Seward needs all the help she can get right now. With the extra guests and visiting servants."

"And yet you are taking time away from your work to play at being a lady's maid and do your hair and write this . . . smut."

Janie's eyes widened. *Smut?*

"The characters you describe are easily recognizable, Janie. And many of them don't come across favorably. Especially the girl who resorts to fisticuffs when she's insulted." Mrs. Griffiths gave Janie a warning look from beneath her brow.

Janie opened her mouth to argue — she'd never been in a fight in her life and was surprised that Charlotte would write about a girl who had.

But Mrs. Griffiths wasn't finished. "Not to mention the sentimental relationships between the men and women. Romantic novels are the territory of Elinor Glyn, not the kitchen maid."

"It's not —" Janie tried to protest, but the housekeeper cut her off.

"You are young, and obviously very impressionable." She restacked the papers and carefully put them back in her desk drawer. "I will keep these. And hope that you will not return to your scribbling. Or your overactive imagination. I would hate to have to show these pages to Lady Diane."

Oh, *no*! The only thing worse than Mrs. Griffiths thinking Janie had written the stories would be Lady Diane *knowing* that Charlotte had. Janie started to speak again, but Mrs. Griffiths wasn't finished.

"So far, I have had no indication that you thought to act on any of these romantic notions," Mrs. Griffiths said, and Janie wondered exactly what Charlotte might have written. "But you know that fraternizing with any staff member of the opposite sex is strictly forbidden."

Janie felt the blush travel from her fingertips all the way to her scalp.

*Lawrence.*

"If I hear one word — *one* — that you are spending time with any boy, much less *kissing* him, I will tell Lady Diane immediately."

Janie looked up into those cold gray eyes. "I'll be sacked."

"Yes, you will be." Mrs. Griffiths didn't sound in the least bit sympathetic.

Who could have found the pages? And who would have handed them to Mrs. Griffiths? Janie wracked her brain. Mollie? Tess?

"You just take care, Janie. It's not only your career on the line here, remember. That is all."

"I promise to do my work efficiently, Mrs. Griffiths," Janie said with a curtsey. "You needn't worry about me wasting my time or kissing anyone."

And she would take care. Of whoever was spying on her.

"See that you do, Janie. See that you do your work and only your work, none of this larking about upstairs. You are a kitchen maid; that's what you're paid to do."

No more Charlotte. Regret pinched behind Janie's eyes.

"Don't frown at me, Janie Seward. You will be watched. You will be judged. And if you do not live up to our standards, you will be leaving The Manor. Forever."

In the course of a single evening, Janie had lost her status in the kitchen, her self-respect, and her friend. She couldn't lose her job and her home, too.

"I understand, Mrs. Griffiths," she said, and left the room.

# Chapter 13

At dinner, Charlotte sat between her youngest brother, Stephen, and Andrew Broadhurst, feeling trapped. Her jaw hurt from clenching it. Far up the table, at the place of precedence on Lord Edmonds's right, Aunt Beatrice didn't look any less miserable. She was dressed in a deep burgundy gown covered in red and gold seed beads in a pattern that swirled like flames. She didn't sit rigidly and austerely like Lady Diane, but almost seemed to slouch into herself.

Charlotte's father didn't notice Aunt Beatrice's reticence. He just talked, and kept saying things like "Isn't that so, Beatrice?" without waiting for a reply.

No one in her family ever waited for a reply.

Charlotte wondered if her aunt really was just at The Manor to steal Mrs. Seward away. Poor Janie.

Lawrence entered with the final course — cheese and fruit and biscuits — and Charlotte felt relief lift her shoulders slightly. She watched him the entire time, but he didn't even look at her. Not once.

His gloved hands carefully laid the plates of cheese on the table, and deftly served the strawberries and plums from another tray to each diner's plate. Charlotte watched his hands, unable to look him in the face for fear everything she felt would be broadcast to the entire table.

"Diane."

Aunt Beatrice's voice was clear and musical. Like a bell.

"Why are you not hosting the servants' ball this year?" Aunt Beatrice asked, suddenly as vibrant as her gown. "Didn't you always have it the night before the first shoot of the season?"

Charlotte stared at her mother. Unlike other great houses, The Manor never had a servants' ball, where the household staff came above stairs and crossed social boundaries to dance with the family.

She imagined herself in Lawrence's arms. In a gown. Almost as if she were at the Season in London. She could see the two of them shocking the entire company with the hesitation waltz.

"We haven't had a servants' ball in years." Lady Diane's tone implied the end of the conversation.

“Why, Mother?” Charlotte heard herself asking.

“Because.” Lady Diane flicked a glance at her sister. “The timing is infelicitous.”

“But we *never* have a servants’ ball,” Charlotte persisted, causing her brothers to shift and prompting David to cough into his sleeve. She knew she shouldn’t be speaking. But she couldn’t stop. “It can’t always be the timing.”

“It is timing and it is planning, Charlotte,” Lady Diane said.

The more her mother argued, the more Charlotte knew it had to happen. It was better than her imagination. It was kismet.

“But the ball is already planned,” she argued. “And it’s just for the houseguests and neighbors, anyway. It doesn’t have to be elaborate.”

Elation swept through her, followed by a hot rush of fear and doubt. Her mother would kill her. Right there on the spot.

“We cannot inconvenience our guests in such a way.” Lady Diane was so stiff her lips hardly moved when she spoke.

“It would be no inconvenience,” Andrew interjected, leaning forward. “I, for one, would be delighted to include your staff.”

Lady Diane stared. Charlotte tried not to. Andrew's face was as bland as ever, but there was mischievous warmth in his dark eyes.

"What a capital idea," Fran said, smiling not-so-discreetly at Lawrence standing on the other side of the room.

Charlotte held her breath.

"Of course, Lord Broadhurst." Lady Diane's face was a mask of indifference.

During the following silence, Charlotte caught Aunt Beatrice smiling and almost grinned in response. It was like they were in cahoots. But she couldn't let Lady Diane think that, so Charlotte kept her expression as blank as possible when she murmured, "Thank you, Mother."

"Very well," Lord Edmonds said. "No need to fuss. And the real action begins with the opening of the shooting season, eh, Lord Broadhurst?" Not pausing for a reply, he added, "Hope the weather's fine."

David made a joke about the heat. Fran joined in with a desire to go to the seaside, which sparked a table-wide discussion about sea-bathing and spa cures, Brighton versus the more local Tunbridge Wells.

"Forgotten again," Charlotte murmured to herself as she sat back in her chair, hands curled in her lap. For just a moment, she had felt as if she was part of the family. Part of the decisions that were made. Part of the discussion.

"Not by all."

Andrew's eyes were even darker in the shadows of the candlelit dining room. Lady Diane hated electric lights over her meal. She said it made the vegetables all look overboiled.

For once, Charlotte was glad of her mother's rules. Andrew looked mysterious. Like he might say something interesting.

"I thought to suggest that you smile," he said, breaking the spell.

Charlotte seethed. She hated to be reminded to smile. Her mother did it all the time.

"But it makes me so irritable when someone suggests it to me," Andrew continued. "It seems . . . false. Forced. And not always welcome."

Charlotte almost lost her voice in surprise.

"Etiquette dictates that we smile even when we don't feel like it," she blurted.

"Society seems to think that no one can ever be sad in public," he said, his thoughtful expression carving sharp angles along his jaw.

"Society sometimes seems to think that we can't even be sad in private," Charlotte quipped, startling herself. Perhaps she was learning something from Janie after all.

Then she remembered to whom she was quipping.

"But no one can be happy all the time. Especially with the way the world is currently," Andrew said.

"What do you mean by that?" Charlotte was uncomfortable having a real conversation with Andrew Broadhurst. She would rather be bored than think any differently of him.

"Take your footman," Andrew said, and indicated Lawrence.

Yes. Charlotte could concentrate on Lawrence.

"He wants more in life than to serve another man's food." Andrew turned back to Charlotte, and at that instant — as if he somehow knew he was no longer being watched by anyone else — Lawrence looked up at her and winked.

"He's been acting as my valet since my early arrival, so I've had a chance to get to know him. He's clever, he's charming, and he reads the papers. And yet, he is not allowed to vote. He's not given a chance to speak his mind because he owns no land and pays no rent."

Charlotte dragged her gaze back to Andrew. "Women aren't allowed to vote, either."

"Exactly!" Andrew exclaimed, and she sat back at his enthusiasm. "What makes me better than Lawrence over there? Or better than you? Nothing."

"Nothing except the circumstances of your birth."

"Which I don't accept as a good enough reason. The greatest injustice is that I never have to work a day in my life, while someone like Lawrence will one day get sick or break a leg and will be out of a job with no food, no doctor, and nothing but squalor to look forward to until he dies."

"Why, Lord Broadhurst." Fran leaned into the conversation from his other side. "You sound like our Chancellor of the Exchequer, trying to guilt us into paying insurance for the working poor. Such talk could get you thrown out of any decent house in the neighborhood."

"Heaven forbid, Miss Caldwell," he said with a chivalrous bow to Fran, who simpered charmingly.

Charlotte thought she might retch.

"I'd never jeopardize my welcome at The Manor," Andrew added. "Which brings me to a question I've been meaning to ask your father, Lady Charlotte. Very important business. Do you know when there might be a good time I can catch him alone?"

Charlotte stifled a gasp. What type of question could Andrew Broadhurst possibly want to ask her father? Especially in private.

Fran's eyebrows looked ready to dance off her face, and Charlotte felt a deep stab in her temple.

"He spends part of every morning in his library," Charlotte said finally.

"Stellar," Andrew said, rubbing his hands together. "I shall endeavor to speak with him before I leave."

When Lady Diane excused the ladies from the table, Charlotte took the opportunity to beg off the obligatory game of bridge.

"I think the heat has given me a headache, Mother," she said quietly as they moved to the sitting room.

Lady Diane's lips turned white — the only indication of her true feelings. The rest of her face was impassive. Possibly — to some — she might appear concerned.

"You don't think you can make up our fourth?" she asked.

Charlotte looked helplessly at the rest of the ladies. Aunt Beatrice. Fran.

Fran smirked.

"We can ask one of the men when they join us," Aunt Beatrice interjected. She smiled at Charlotte. Actually smiled, and her eyes held true concern. "It's probably best that Charlotte feel entirely herself for the shooting party. A good night's sleep will do her no harm."

"What do you know about raising children?" Lady Diane snapped, startling them all.

"Nothing." Aunt Beatrice's face fell into the same unreadable expression as her sister's. "Obviously. I just know that sleep often cures me."

"And responsibility? Social mores? They count for nothing, do they?" Lady Diane asked, her voice a hiss in the quiet sitting room. Fran stood with her back to them, a book in front of her. But Charlotte knew she heard every word they spoke.

"Sometimes, one has to decide what is best for everyone," Aunt Beatrice said quietly.

Lady Diane suddenly seemed to realize that Charlotte still stood at her elbow. She waved an apathetic hand.

"Go, then. Ring Sarah if you need anything."

A servant. Not a mother. Not even a friend. No one really to care for her.

Except for Janie.

Charlotte immediately asked for Janie when Sarah answered the bell, but the housemaid just shook her head and said Janie couldn't come upstairs.

"What do you mean?" Charlotte asked. Now she really was getting a headache.

"She's needed in the kitchen, Lady Charlotte." Sarah dipped a curtsey.

Was she imagining it, or did Sarah smirk?

Sarah efficiently helped her out of her evening dress, unlaced her corset, handed her a dressing gown. Then sat her down in front of a mirror to undo her hair.

Charlotte studied the housemaid's face in the mirror. It was a pure blank, as if she were purposefully holding something back.

Or telling a fib.

Charlotte pressed her fingers to her temples.

"I did so want to talk to her."

Sarah harrumphed. "About what? How to roast a leg of mutton?"

"I do think that's unfair, Sarah."

The housemaid's mouth straightened out into a firm line and she tugged perhaps a little too harshly on Charlotte's hair.

"Stop." Charlotte reached up and took the brush out of Sarah's hand. "Just stop. I have a headache. Please send Janie up with something hot."

"I will bring it to you, Lady Charlotte."

"No." Charlotte used a tone that was firmer than any of the servants were used to. Sarah looked a little shocked, but hid it quickly. Charlotte found she didn't care. "I want a warm cloth. I want tea. And I want Janie."

Sarah appeared about to say something but Charlotte silenced her with a look. Such an immediate response made Charlotte feel powerful.

Charlotte wasn't sure she liked it, this feeling of dominance. It felt . . . wrong. But at least it worked. Sarah left without another word, and Charlotte arranged herself on her bed. Trying to look as if her head really hurt. She imagined her mother worrying about her. Coming upstairs to see what was wrong. Only to find Charlotte slipping away into a faint, never to recover.

Charlotte put the back of her hand to her forehead and assumed a tragic expression.

There was a swift, purposeful knock at the door and she waited a moment.

"Come in," she said weakly.

"You don't sound like you have a headache." Janie entered with a warm compress and a pot of tea.

Charlotte sat up and flung the counterpane to the floor.

"I just couldn't stand another minute in that room with those people."

"They're your people."

Charlotte nodded, and patted the edge of her bed. Janie perched, twisting her hands in her lap.

"I need your help," Charlotte whispered.

"I don't think I can help you anymore," Janie said. Charlotte could clearly see the dark smudges beneath her eyes.

"It's important."

A crease appeared between Janie's eyebrows. Charlotte almost laughed. She had one exactly like it when she was writing or thinking. Lady Diane always reprimanded her for it.

"Is . . . is someone in trouble?" Janie asked.

Charlotte wondered if she could trust Janie enough to tell her about the kiss with Lawrence. About how it seemed to go on forever and be over in an instant.

"Is it one of the staff?" Janie asked. She looked truly worried. "Have you heard something that could get someone dismissed?"

Charlotte put a cool hand to her cheek. Lawrence could be dismissed.

"No," she said carefully. "It's Andrew Broadhurst."

Charlotte paused, and Janie stayed silent, waiting for her to continue. It was refreshing. Fran was always waiting to jump into the conversation, just like Charlotte's father and brothers. It was like they weren't really listening to her words but for an opportunity to speak their own. Janie actually heard what Charlotte wanted to say.

"I need to know what he's planning to ask my father."

"Oh." Janie's eyes widened in understanding.

"You see my problem," Charlotte said quickly, clambering out of bed. She went to stand by the window, the darkness outside almost impenetrable. She thought of the lightheartedness of Andrew's expression. The secret mirth that she found she wanted to share. She shook the thought away.

"Do you think he's going to ask for your hand?" Janie stood behind her. "Soon?"

Charlotte nodded. The ghost of her reflection nodded in the wavy glass.

"Does he even know you?" Janie asked. "Or is he just doing what's expected? What *his* mother tells him to?"

There was an edge to Janie's voice. An edge that Charlotte didn't like. Almost as if Janie were talking not about Andrew Broadhurst, but about someone else. Someone who always did what was expected. Who never went against her mother's wishes.

Suddenly, Charlotte wanted to prove that she wasn't that person. She was someone who would try a hot chili pepper. Someone who could be adventurous.

"I kissed him, Janie."

"Lord Broadhurst?" Janie sounded appropriately shocked, and Charlotte considered going along with the lie. But she wanted someone to know the truth.

"Lawrence."

Janie looked like she had swallowed an Indian chili whole.

"No, you didn't." She shook her head. "You've been with Miss Caldwell the whole time."

Charlotte turned around to face her. "I kissed him before tea. I left Fran on the patio, and said I was going to order chocolate cakes. But I found him in the footman's closet and I kissed him."

"Please don't tell me that," Janie said. She sounded like she had that chili stuck in her throat. Like it had burned her.

"Who else am I going to tell?" Charlotte said. "Fran? *Mother?* You're the only friend I have who might understand, Janie!"

"I don't think I do understand. I don't think you do, either."

"I think I'm in love with him," Charlotte said with more conviction than she felt. "And that's all that matters."

"You're not —" Janie stopped.

"Not what, Janie?" Charlotte glared at her. "Not in love with him? Not *worthy* of him?"

"I don't think he loves you."

"Why?"

"Because he tried to kiss me, too."

All the air left Charlotte's lungs and roared around her ears. She could taste spite like venom on her tongue. "I think you're jealous. Not because I live in the big house and sleep in a big bed and have silks and furs and all the rest. You're not like that."

Janie didn't reply.

"You think you're so much better because you have a career," Charlotte continued, her own bitterness turning her stomach sour. "You have a goal. Something to work for. Something to *do*, and all I accomplish is sitting around and writing letters and paying calls and waiting to get married."

Janie shook her head.

"You can have everything!" Charlotte sobbed, realizing it was true. That Janie wasn't the one who was jealous at all. "Freedom, a job, a purpose, a *mother.* And you wanted the only thing that could be mine.

"You already had love," Charlotte finished, "and you wanted his, too."

"You can't live on love."

"Spoken like a true cynic." Charlotte felt the bitterness rise up again.

"No," Janie said. "Spoken like a realist. As soon as your mother finds out, he'll be sacked. With no pay and no reference. And then what will you do?"

"He'll work somewhere else."

"Now that's where you're wrong," Janie said. "When word gets out that Lawrence seduced the daughter of The Manor, he will be barred from every decent house in England. He will be blacklisted."

"We'll make it, as long as we're together." But doubt had started to creep into Charlotte's mind.

"Will you?" Janie asked quietly. "When my father died and my mother went back into service, I lived in a two-room cottage with my grandmother, my aunt and uncle, and seven cousins. My uncle worked the farm. My two older cousins were lookerers — shepherds on the Romney Marsh. And the rest of us just starved."

"Don't be overdramatic, Janie," Charlotte sneered.

"One meal a day, Charlotte. Sometimes just a potato. Or cabbage soup. Is that what you want? And if you think you can handle it, is that what you want for him? Do you love him enough to make him starve for you?"

Did she?

"We wouldn't . . ."

"You might," Janie said quietly, and Charlotte saw tears in her eyes. "Is it really worth the risk?"

"But you are the risk taker, Janie. You're the one who tried the Indian chili first. You leapt headfirst off of the ha-ha."

"I broke my collarbone," Janie said with a dry laugh. "And when it gets cold and damp, I can still feel it, because it didn't set right. I couldn't stop working, Charlotte, or I would lose my place. I would do everything to prevent my ever going back to the life I once lived.

"Which is why I *thought* about kissing Lawrence," she went on, and Charlotte could see she told the truth. "But I never would. Life isn't a romantic novel, and it's certainly not poetry. Only stories have the happily-ever-after."

Janie's face hardened until it looked like she was wearing a mask.

"I'm not your friend, Charlotte. I am your maid. Your *servant*. And I will not be privy to your secrets."

"Then go back to your kitchen," Charlotte snapped.

Charlotte felt the room go still around her. Janie didn't even breathe. But she dropped her hands and left the room, shutting the door silently behind her.

# Chapter 14

Guilt sat heavily on Janie's chest, slowing her down and cramping her fingers. All through the morning, it threatened to consume her. Through the boiling kettle and the too-sticky porridge, through the burned scones and bitter coffee and complaints. Only the sharp chiming of the bells roused her from her stupor.

Upstairs and downstairs were divided. By rules and bells and baize-covered doors. Maybe what she'd said was true — maybe she and Charlotte couldn't be friends. But that didn't mean she didn't care.

Lawrence could lose his job for kissing Charlotte. But Charlotte could lose her social standing. Her reputation. The very life she led.

Janie couldn't let that happen.

When she saw Lawrence enter the butler's pantry alone, she slipped in after him.

"What do you think you're playing at?" Janie hissed. "With Lady Charlotte?"

Lawrence wouldn't look at her. He tried to get around her, but she didn't move.

"Nothing, Janie." Lawrence offered her one of his disarming smiles, and she wanted to slap it off his face.

"Charlotte doesn't think it's nothing."

"*Lady* Charlotte was just —"

"Just what, Lawrence? Just in your way? Just trying to *kiss* you?"

The smile disappeared, and his eyes glittered. "You certainly don't beat around the bush, Janie."

"I see no reason to! You're ruining her."

A ghost of the smile returned. "Calm down."

Lawrence's condescending tone made Janie livid. "If anyone else had seen that. Lady Diane. Miss Caldwell. Lord Broadhurst. All of Charlotte's chances would be bankrupted. She'd never marry."

Lawrence raised an eyebrow. "Marriage to the aristocracy isn't the ultimate goal."

"It is for them!" Janie flung her hand up to indicate the upper floors of The Manor. "It's all they've got, Lawrence. If she doesn't marry, what does she have left? She's not strong and she's not brave, and she couldn't survive in the outside world."

The guilt returned like a kick in the chest because Janie wasn't telling the truth. Charlotte ate that chili without sputtering or spewing. Charlotte wrote her life into her stories, making it different from what it was. She did have a hidden strength. She did have something more. Something not visible in the pale skin and innocent hazel eyes.

"She's rich," Lawrence said. "She'll be fine."

"What about you?" Janie said, grasping. "You're jeopardizing your position here. Your whole career."

That got his attention. For the first time, he looked a little less than confident. So Janie pushed her advantage.

"You think there's no blacklist for servants? We all know who *not* to work for. We have our own network — *Oh, don't work for Lord Doolally because he never pays wages* — and Lord D suddenly has no staff. You think it doesn't work the other way?"

"You don't know everything," Lawrence said. He deftly stepped to the side to get around her, but Janie followed him. Dogging him.

"I know everything there is to know about this manor and the people who live in it," Janie said.

"That's where you're wrong, Janie." Lawrence stopped and

finally looked at her, his mouth straightening into a firm line. "There's more to people than what you see on the surface."

Janie remembered what she had thought of Charlotte just a few days before. Spoiled. Cosseted. Ready to do whatever was expected.

"Maybe you're right," she said quietly.

"Things are changing, Janie. It's inevitable." Lawrence offered one last smile. She no longer found it charming. "Don't get left behind."

After he left, Janie leaned against the wall beneath the bells. She wondered if the world could change enough for two people to kiss without dire consequences. A world where a lady could be a writer or a king could marry a commoner. Where stepping out of place wouldn't get you knocked down.

By midmorning, the basement was full of dust and guns and leather trunks crammed with enough dresses to change four or five times a day. And servants. Party guests required maids and valets and coachmen.

All the talk was of the ball. The *servants'* ball.

"Are we all invited?" Lord Buckden's valet asked, leaning against the kitchen doorjamb. His thick Highland brogue made him difficult to understand. But at least he was talking to her. Unlike The Manor staff. Tess had left the first batch of bread to burn. And Mollie had taken to leaving pots caked with food in the middle of Janie's work area.

"I believe so," Janie said, mixing fat into flour for the pie dough. "We've never had a servants' ball before."

The way everyone was acting toward her, she wasn't sure she wanted to go.

Janie surveyed the mess in the kitchen and sighed.

"Only a few more hours, sweeting," Mrs. Seward said, bustling in past the now-retreating valet. "The servants will have their supper early, and we can clean up before the ball. I'll have Mollie help."

"You think I'm trying to get out of my work now, too?" Janie snapped.

"I just thought you might be tired." Mrs. Seward went to the other side of the table, where a piece of beef waited to be filleted.

"Who cares if I'm tired?" Janie said. "You're tired. Mollie's tired. The housemaids are tired. I'm not trying to get out of anything, and I'm certainly not saying I'm better than anyone else."

"Has someone been implying this?"

The kitchen — and its staff — was Mrs. Seward's domain. But when the last kitchen maid got caught with the chauffeur, it was Mrs. Griffiths who did the sacking. Janie's mother would have given the girl another chance. And Mrs. Griffiths knew it. Which was why the housekeeper had taken Janie into her sitting room alone.

And why Janie couldn't get her mother involved.

"I can handle it."

"You can't be in two places at once," her mother said. "The entire place is overrun with the shooting party and the ball, and there you are traipsing upstairs to do hair as if you were a little girl with her dolls."

"Well, you don't have to worry about that anymore." Janie felt her throat begin to close and turned away, swiping ineffectually at the flour Tess had spilled across the floor. "I know where I belong. In this kitchen."

"Maybe you do," Mrs. Seward said, her thin, sharp knife moving deftly, swiftly, but never touching her fingers. "Like I do. Just maybe not *this* kitchen."

Janie's throat felt too thick to reply. Her mother was planning to leave. Janie looked around. At the scarred table. The brick floor, worn smooth around the stove where someone almost always stood — and always had — stirring and frying and cooking. At the gleaming copper pots hanging from their pegs. At the still-dirty ones under the sink. At the flour still on the floor.

She'd always assumed she belonged here. She could feel it in her bones. But did she deserve better? Is that what her mother was talking about?

The servants' entrance thumped open, and footsteps clattered on the brick floor of the kitchen corridor.

It sounded like a herd of wild animals coming into the house.

Janie looked up and met her mother's eye. Mrs. Seward covered the beef with a plate and came around the table to kiss her on the forehead.

"You belong wherever your heart is," she said, and stepped into the hall and was swallowed up by the chaos.

Janie turned out the dough for the pies, filling each one with meat and gravy. The noise from the corridor rose to near-deafening proportions as the new staff called out questions about locked cases and where to unpack and if there was any shoe black available. Janie couldn't imagine being in the middle of it without her mother. Without her support. Without that kiss on her forehead.

She was decorating the tops of each pie with leaves of pastry when Tess stomped into the kitchen and slammed an ice-cream churn in front of her on the floor.

"I don't have time for this," Tess said, her face red, her expression indignant.

Janie went back to the pastry leaves. "It's too hot for ices."

"Not according to Lady Diane. If there's ice in the ice-house, ice cream can be made!"

Tess walked out, her back straight with arrogance. Janie looked down at the can of cream, at the condensation that gathered on the metal lid. The chunks of ice in the bucket were melting rapidly.

"Blast."

Janie put the pies in the oven and took the ice-cream churn to the larder, where at least it was marginally cooler. Both for the ice cream and herself.

She faced the wood block where the pheasants were plucked. And the rack where the strings of birds would hang up over it. Thank goodness the shooting hadn't begun, or Mollie would be in here with her, plucking the birds. She took a deep breath to suppress the tears before they overwhelmed her. She knelt on the floor to crank the ice cream.

She didn't turn when she heard footsteps behind her.

"Janie," Harry said, coming into the room and looking into the wooden cupboards. "I'm to take some eggs to Mr. Foyle; he's supposed to make some kind of cocktail that Lord Buckden has asked for. Something ridiculous he drinks at his club that's made with raw eggs, syrup, and brandy. Do you know where they — Janie? Are you all right?"

Janie refused to look at him.

"The eggs are over there in the corner," she said. "They got moved to make room for the birds."

Harry squatted down next to where she struggled to turn the arm of the ice-cream churn.

"Let me do that."

"You have your own job to do."

Janie pushed again at the churn, and it barely moved.

"Cocktail hour isn't until six," Harry said, putting his hand on hers. "Here, you sit on the churn and I'll turn the handle."

Janie turned her back to him to sit on the top of the churn. She gathered up her skirts around her and buried her face in them. She felt the churn move a little and widened her stance to keep it from sliding across the floor. The metal can of ice cream creaked and began to spin slowly and sporadically.

"Isn't this almost done?" Harry panted.

"Only when you can't move it anymore."

"Won't it all melt before pudding is served?"

"Probably."

"Is that what has you crying?"

Janie sighed. "I don't cry."

"It's true, Janie Seward. Not even when you broke your collarbone. There's not much that can make you cry. Whatever's got you this close must be pretty bad."

Janie turned her head slightly, to see him out of her peripheral vision. To feel his breath on her cheek.

Harry stopped churning and stood up, pulling her up with him. He stood with one hand on each of her shoulders and waited until she looked up into his face.

Janie wasn't sure how long they stood there. She felt the atmosphere shift around her. The heat of his hands on her arms. The intensity of his gaze.

Janie shook her head. This was *Harry.* And she was not some infatuated girl. Not like Charlotte chasing a footman. She moved away and busied herself with the ice-cream churn: unbuckling the hand crank, pulling the canister out of the bucket, and placing it on the cool stone floor. She pulled up the dasher from the center of the can and inspected it.

"My ma is going to work for Lady Beatrice," she finally said.

As soon as she said it, Janie wished she hadn't. Saying it out loud made it seem so real. A real coup for Lady Beatrice, getting a great cook and stealing her from her sister. A real loss for The Manor. For Janie.

"You're leaving?"

Janie dipped a finger into the soft ice cream and put it in her mouth. Closed her eyes, the sweetness spreading over her tongue.

"I don't think I'm invited." Janie didn't open her eyes, enjoying the anonymity of the cool darkness behind the lids. "And I don't think I want to leave."

"You always said you'd stay here forever, Janie, but being a lady's maid would mean leaving. Going with Lady Charlotte. Or someone else. She's not going to stay here forever."

Janie put the lid back on the canister and finally looked at him. "I don't really want to be a lady's maid. But it was . . . fun. Pretending. Going upstairs. It's so pretty, Harry. Those paintings on the walls and the carpets beneath your feet."

"Even when they don't belong to you?" Harry asked.

"You don't have to own beauty to appreciate it."

"Don't you want more, Janie?" Harry asked. He sounded like he expected her to. "From your life? You're so smart . . . you could be a writer or something."

Janie almost laughed. Where on earth had Harry gotten that idea? But then she remembered. Harry had seen her with Charlotte's papers. He was the only person who knew about them.

And *someone* told Mrs. Griffiths.

"Or is it something else?" Harry continued, his voice hoarse. "Or *someone* . . . you want to stay here for?"

Harry must have seen her *almost* kiss Lawrence. Harry,

who could move through the entire house without a sound because it was his job. Harry, who was . . .

Jealous?

"It was you," Janie said.

A torrent of emotions crossed Harry's face, so quickly Janie could only guess what was behind them. Fear. Confusion. Excitement. Relief.

*Guilt.*

The pain of his betrayal was so swift and so sharp that Janie almost cried out. He took a step toward her, and she thrust out her hands to force him back.

"Don't talk to me about what I want, Harry Peasgood, because in the end you're just like everyone else. *Stay in your place, Janie Seward, you don't deserve to want anything else.*"

"Ah, Janie, please don't be like that." Harry stared at her. He looked confused.

Janie advanced on him, her anger rising, obliterating her grief. She approached him as she imagined a tiger would. Carefully. Menacingly.

"Don't be like what, Harry?"

"Like this. Like you're mad at me. I don't understand what I said."

"It's what you said and what you *did.*"

"What do you mean?"

"You *know* I'd never do anything to jeopardize my position here, and yet you did it for me."

Harry's eyes grew round. "I don't understand."

"You do understand, Harry. You're the only one who does. The only one who knows what this place means to me, and the only one who knows what I will lose if I'm sacked. Because I won't just be losing a job, will I?"

"Janie —"

"So don't worry, Harry. Point taken. I will not step another toe out of line, because I can't afford to lose this place. Not now. Not ever."

"I know all this, Janie!"

"Then why did you do it?" Janie cried. "Why? How could you?"

Real fear careened across his face. And real concern galloped after it. He reached for her, but she ducked away. But he caught her around the middle and wrapped his arms around her, his chest pressed tight to her back.

"What did I do, Janie?" he murmured in her ear. "I don't know how to make it right."

Janie stopped struggling and looked up at him over her shoulder. Remembering the night he watched the stars, and she had seen them reflected in his eyes.

"Why do I have to tell you?" she asked. It didn't come out

as angrily as she intended. It came out soft and questioning. Pleading, almost.

"Because I want to help." The tone of his voice and the way he looked directly into her eyes almost had her convinced. She wanted to believe him.

"Why?" she asked.

"Because I . . ." Harry never took his eyes off her face.

Out of the corner of her eye, Janie saw Mrs. Griffiths appear in the doorway, shock shadowing her features. Janie tried to pull away from Harry, but he held her too tightly.

"No," Janie whispered, but the housekeeper cut across her.

"Mr. Foyle is asking about those eggs, Harry."

Harry dropped his arms as if he held a living coal in them and stepped abruptly backward, knocking over the bucket of salty water.

"No!" Janie cried again.

She watched as Harry stumbled a second time, tipping over the ice-cream canister with its sticky, melting contents. Brushing the half dozen eggs he'd collected off the table and onto the floor. She watched as Mrs. Griffiths marched him out of the larder and up into the kitchen courtyard.

She watched as her entire world fell apart around her, knowing there was nothing she could do to keep it together.

# Chapter 15

Charlotte stood at the top of the grand staircase in her first Worth gown. The silk dress was a deep, rich green. The hem was slightly raised in the front, showing a shimmery gold underdress, a hint of ankle, and her slippers dyed to match, with a bit of a train in the back.

The bodice of the gown was beaded in a geometrical pattern, jet and glass beads that sparkled when they caught the light. And a huge silk rose on the shoulder strap held the little chiffon demi-sleeves, the pale green silk almost like sea foam.

Normally, such a dress would be purchased for a girl's first Season. She'd be presented at court and then attend countless balls in a series of equally stunning gowns, hoping to attract a proposal. It was quite a coup to get an offer during the debut year.

Lady Diane had told Charlotte on their shopping trip in Paris that she hoped for a proposal before Charlotte was ever presented at court. She hinted that Charlotte shouldn't expect many more of these gowns. At least not any purchased on the Edmonds's account.

Charlotte knew that meant only one thing. That Lady Diane wanted her daughter out of The Manor and off her hands. And that this dress was intended to beguile Andrew Broadhurst. Tonight.

Charlotte imagined herself in the shimmering, sealike gown on the balcony of a hotel on the Côte d'Azur in France. Lawrence could be a painter — someone modern and passionate, like that Picasso. And Charlotte would write all day. Books about adventure and airplanes. Or maybe books about the English aristocracy. Making fun of their extravagances. Bridging the gap between the classes.

She would prove Janie wrong.

She laid a gloved hand on the gleaming stair rail. She knew it was dusted and polished daily while the family was at lunch or out riding. She rarely saw the maids who did it. Everything at The Manor ran with precision and grace. Invisibly. So she could appear at the top of the stairs — a perfect vision.

Charlotte glanced down and saw that the marble hall was empty. She was earlier even than Lady Diane, who usually waited for her dinner guests at the bottom of the staircase. Charlotte hesitated one more moment, and then decided to go back to her room and count to twenty before coming out again.

Charlotte turned and almost ran headlong into Andrew Broadhurst's chest. With a little cry, she stepped backward. The heel of her shoe connected with nothing but air and she teetered over the precipice of the grand staircase — only the checkered marble at the bottom to stop her fall.

Andrew slipped an arm around her waist and pulled her upright. The lapels of his dinner jacket gleamed dully, his white tie just a tiny bit out of alignment. He smelled of sandalwood and spice.

"I didn't mean to startle you," he said, his voice rumbling against her. "Are you all right?"

Charlotte looked up into his eyes — darker than ever in the dim light of the staircase.

"I'm fine," she said quickly, then remembered herself. "Thank you."

Andrew turned, guiding her away from the stairs, and then let her go. Like a gentleman, he stepped back, leaving an appropriate amount of space between them.

"Were you going down?" he asked.

"No." Charlotte couldn't look him in the face. Couldn't look into those eyes.

"Of course not. You were about to leave." He stepped to the side to allow her to pass.

"No," Charlotte said. "I mean, yes. I was going downstairs. I just . . . realized I was early. And thought I should wait."

"Let's wait together, shall we?"

Charlotte's thoughts still churned with daydreams. Being a writer. Standing at the Côte d'Azur with a handsome man at her side.

"What are the other men doing?" she asked.

"Cocktails," Andrew said. "Lord Buckden has become quite a connoisseur at his club, apparently."

"And you're not joining them?"

"Not when more stimulating company presents itself."

Andrew grinned at her. He seemed so . . . charming.

"Besides," he continued, leaning forward to murmur into her ear, his cinnamon-scented breath fluttering the hair at her temple, "the thought of trying to swallow something made of raw eggs, crushed ice, brandy, and milk is enough to make me swear off the stuff forever."

Charlotte made an appropriately disgusted face and

finally looked into his eyes. They were a rich, chocolaty brown, but contained flickers of light like chips of gold. And again, she felt they shared a common joke at the expense of the rest of the aristocracy.

"Surely it would be an adventure," she finally managed, and edged her words with a tease. "A new taste thrill."

"I think I prefer to get my adventure elsewhere," Andrew replied. "Travel. Making my own way. Running my own business."

Oh, dear. Business sounded dreadfully dull. Charlotte tried hard not to yawn.

"Airplanes."

"Flying?" she asked, her voice a squeak.

Andrew laughed. "It's every bit as frightening as you think, but equally thrilling."

Charlotte tried to imagine what it would be like to look down upon the trees and valleys around The Manor. She was astonished at how easy it was to imagine Andrew Broadhurst flying the plane.

"I'm shocked, Lord Broadhurst," she said with a genuine smile.

"I'm afraid I want more out of life than just garden parties and village fetes."

"I do, as well," Charlotte blurted in surprise. "I just feel like the world is changing, and I want to be there to see it. To be a part of it."

Andrew cocked his head and looked at her, but was silent for so long, Charlotte began to feel she had shocked him. Offended him.

"And how do you want to do that?" he asked finally.

At first, she thought he might be mocking her. When she was little and expressed opinions, her brothers used to throw them back at her. Teasing and jibing until she cried.

Andrew looked like he really wanted to know the answer.

"I'd like to be a writer," she said. And immediately regretted it. She'd never told anyone about her writing. Except Janie. Who was no longer her friend.

"A journalist?" Andrew asked.

Charlotte thought of Nellie Bly, who had pretended to be insane to expose the cruel treatment of madwomen in a New York asylum. And had later gone on to travel around the world in fewer than eighty days. She didn't just write about adventure, she lived it. She didn't just think about change, she created it.

It sounded terrifying.

She could let him think this of her. She imagined that she was plucky and audacious and worthy of admiration. But

Charlotte was surprised by how much she wanted him to know the truth.

"I write fiction," she admitted. "Stories. Adventures."

Andrew smiled amusedly. "About what?"

Charlotte frowned. "Are you patronizing me?"

Andrew became all seriousness. "Not at all, Lady Charlotte. It's obviously something about which you feel passionate, and I respect that. In fact, I admire it very much. It's something to which we should all aspire."

"And what's that?"

"Doing something we love."

Warmth spread through her at how well he understood. Only to be replaced by coldness when she saw Fran approaching from the far end of the hall.

"What are you two waiting for?" Fran called. "Me?" She slipped a slim arm around Charlotte's and whispered in her ear, "Has he proposed yet?"

More loudly, she added, "You shouldn't have."

"We didn't," Charlotte blurted, and Fran dropped her arm, glaring. Andrew coughed.

"Really, Charlotte," Fran said. "It's no wonder your mother wants to send you to finishing school."

Charlotte steeled herself to make a response, but Andrew stepped between them.

"I must be the luckiest man in the world to escort two such fetching young ladies to dinner," he said. His voice was different. Back to its upper-class, Eton-educated tones. Charlotte realized this switch expertly doused the animosity between the two girls.

"May I?" Andrew held out one arm to Fran and extended the other to Charlotte, who took it gratefully, and the three of them headed down the stairs.

"Looking forward to the servants' ball?" Andrew asked.

"I'm sure Charlotte is," Fran said.

Charlotte felt a flush of embarrassment, followed quickly by anger at Fran for being so casual with her secrets.

"Yes," she stuttered.

"It must be such a treat for them," Fran continued. "To be able to experience the way the other half lives."

She sounded so condescending, Charlotte considered turning around and going back to bed. If this was how the rest of the guests would act, it would be a flaming embarrassment to be among them.

"I think it is more of a gift for the rest of us," Andrew said. "To be able to spend an evening in the company of our fellow man."

Fran laughed. "I think you have to sit by me again this

evening, Lord Broadhurst. I shall have need of your diverting remarks."

The dinner seemed to go on forever. Course after course — twelve rather than five. Charlotte thought of poor Janie down in the kitchen. Mrs. Seward rushed off her feet. None of them would want to dance after all that. One would think they'd just want to go to bed.

And the one time she thought she might be interested in talking more with Andrew Broadhurst, he was placed farther down the table, diverting Fran. And Charlotte was stuck between her brother Stephen and Lord Buckden, who appeared to have fallen asleep over the cheese, which was a blessing. He only mumbled when he talked, with a tendency to spray.

Stephen just ignored her entirely.

But Lawrence didn't. Though he moved with absolute decorum and served silently and efficiently, she felt his eyes on her. She imagined that he was as anxious for their dance together as she was. She tried to picture the hesitation waltz. Instead, she saw herself dancing with Andrew Broadhurst, and shook the thought away.

Aunt Beatrice was quiet throughout the meal, tucked between Charlotte's father and Lord Ellis. She was the very picture of "speak only when spoken to," and therefore didn't speak at all. She wore a soft gray dress, the black ribbons and beads soothing rather than fiery. It was like she didn't want to be seen.

Charlotte wished she'd had a chance to talk to her aunt. Surely Aunt Beatrice would prefer to be in Italy or America or wherever she was going next. The Manor must be stifling. There was nothing for her here.

When dinner was over and the ladies moved to the sitting room for coffee, Fran swept up beside Charlotte and wrapped an arm around her waist.

"I saw you," she whispered into Charlotte's ear. Her hair tickled the same way it had when Andrew had spoken to her, but this felt more like an omen.

Charlotte tried to pull away, but Fran wouldn't let her.

"Watching the footman all night, weren't you? I wouldn't let it go too far if I were you."

"Well, you're not me, are you?" Charlotte snapped.

"No." Fran turned bitter eyes on her. "You've always been the good girl. You would never risk losing everything. Your family. Your reputation."

"What about love?"

Fran navigated them around a spindly tea table and into the far corner of the room. "Is love really worth losing all of this?" She waved her hand at the sitting room, The Manor, the yawning fireplace.

"None of this is mine," Charlotte said. "I'm just a tenant."

"You're being purposefully obtuse. It's the *idea* of it all I'm talking about. You think you want to give this up for a rented semidetached cottage in Surrey? For a man who stinks of coal soot? Mending your own clothes and — God forbid — cooking your own dinners? I can't even make my own toast, Charlotte!"

"You sound like you're proud of that."

"I am! I'm rich and well-bred, and I can pay someone to make my toast and bring me tea. I wouldn't give that up for anything."

Charlotte didn't know how to make toast, either. She could have tried to learn from Janie, but that didn't mean she would have been any good at it.

"Personally," Fran added, "I'm not giving up my silks and servants."

"What about your dreams?"

"I'm not a dreamer, Charlotte. I'm a realist. And if you persist in being off in the clouds, you're going to find that it's raining in your reality."

"What does that mean?" Charlotte didn't think she could stand one more moment in Fran's company.

"It means Andrew Broadhurst won't be looking at you with those puppy-dog eyes for long," Fran said with a tight smile. "Maybe someone else will snap him up."

"Like you?" Charlotte hissed. "What about David?"

Not that Charlotte relished the idea of Fran marrying her brother. But the idea of Fran with Andrew somehow rankled Charlotte even more.

"Carrying on with this childish infatuation will not only bring you down, Charlotte, it will destroy your family." Fran looked at her pointedly. "I don't wish to marry into a family on the verge of scandal. And I doubt Lord Broadhurst will, either."

Fran turned and swished away, the flare of her pink handkerchief hem rustling on the carpet.

"You can have him," Charlotte muttered under her breath. But felt a little jolt of conscience, right beneath the growing lump of dread lodged against her breastbone.

When they reentered the marble hall, it had been transformed. Swags of greenery and flowers traveled down the grand staircase, and tall pillar candles lit the back corners. The front doors had been opened to the soft whisper of the fading daylight — stars just visible above the inky hedgerows and the yellow moon rising on the eastern horizon.

Lawrence stood just inside the door, almost silhouetted against the sky, watching the other servants arrive. They looked awkward in their Sunday best. Compared to the showy silks and glittering jewels of the guests, the maids' bright cotton dresses looked drab. Even Mrs. Griffiths's best black silk looked muted in comparison.

Tess, the head kitchen maid, had plaited her hair into an elaborate crown. Even Mollie the scullery girl had cleaned up a bit, and hid her chapped hands behind her back. Charlotte frowned when she didn't see Janie.

Lord Edmonds stepped forward to address them.

"Welcome," he said to the guests, then turned to the servants. "Welcome, all. This is a tradition we haven't kept for a long time." He paused, his eyes traveling to Lady Diane, then lighting briefly on Lady Beatrice. "But one we hope will carry happy relationships into the future."

Charlotte sighed. Her father was so good at making speeches.

Just not very good at personal conversations.

Everyone arranged themselves — the guests on one side of the room, servants on the other, like opposing teams at a cricket match. Charlotte placed herself somewhere near the middle. She wasn't quite ready to choose one side or the other.

"I wanted to thank you, Lady Charlotte," Sarah said, sidling up to stand next to her.

"What for?"

"For the ball. We heard it was your doing." Sarah leaned forward to whisper over Charlotte's shoulder. "Occasionally, we have a little dance downstairs. The chauffeur plays the piano. And sometimes the gardener's boy comes in with a fiddle." She raised her eyebrows as if divulging a great secret.

"Do you?" Charlotte asked, remembering Sarah in the basement hall behind Mrs. Griffiths. "And who do you dance with?"

Sarah hesitated.

"Go on, Sarah." Charlotte smiled encouragingly. "I won't tell."

"The new footman, my lady," Sarah said. "Lawrence. He's mighty handsome, that one."

Charlotte's throat squeezed shut. Of course Lawrence had danced with Sarah. Lawrence danced with everyone. He'd even said Janie promised him a dance.

Janie.

She was jealous. That's why she'd said those horrid things to Charlotte. Because Charlotte had kissed Lawrence first.

Janie said Lawrence had almost kissed her, too. Charlotte swallowed.

"It's the talk of the downstairs, my lady," Sarah said.

For a moment, Charlotte wondered if Janie's jealousy was the talk of the downstairs. Or, God forbid, her own indiscretions. Maybe Janie had told. Maybe everyone knew.

"What is?" she breathed.

"The ball," Sarah said, her eyes meeting Charlotte's.

Charlotte saw a spark in the maid's expression.

"That and the kitchen maid," Sarah said. Her voice was casual. Offhand. As if it were something Charlotte would know about already. As if it wasn't worth mentioning.

"The kitchen maid?" Charlotte prompted.

"Janie," Sarah said, her face impassive. Watching the musicians tune up.

"What about her?"

"Why, she's been sacked, of course," Sarah said. "Consorting with one of the men."

Charlotte almost stopped breathing.

"Which one?"

Sarah leaned forward again, her eyes alight with gossip and mischief.

"The hall boy," Sarah said, scandalized. "Harry Peasgood."

Memories tumbled around in Charlotte's mind. Harry daring Janie to eat the Indian chili. The way he watched Janie when he thought no one was looking.

Sarah must have taken Charlotte's silence as enticement to elaborate. "Mrs. Griffiths found them in the larder," the housemaid said. "In a frightful clinch. Mind you, that boy has been mooning after her for years, she was just too thick to see it."

"Or didn't want to," Charlotte said quietly.

Janie wouldn't risk her job. Not even for Harry.

But she had risked her job to help Charlotte. To keep her secrets.

The musicians started up a waltz and the hall resonated with the music. The room had originally been the Tudor-era great hall, and must have seen a great many dances. Charlotte couldn't help but feel that this one was not going to go as she imagined.

She wondered if she should sneak downstairs and find Janie. If Janie hadn't already left The Manor for good. She watched Lady Diane, whose face was a mask of disinterest. Almost boredom.

And Charlotte realized she didn't need to find Janie.

She needed to talk to her mother.

While the guests and servants stood and stared at one another uncomfortably, Charlotte strode across the checkered floor and stopped in front of Lady Diane.

"Mother, I need to speak with you."

Lady Diane narrowed her eyes. "Not now, Charlotte. We have guests."

"We can speak about this privately," Charlotte pursued, with more confidence in her voice than she felt. "Or we can speak about this here. But speak about it, I will."

Lady Diane's lips went white with anger.

"Very well, Charlotte, come into my sitting room."

A surge of triumph pushed Charlotte forward. As she followed her mother, she pictured herself telling Lady Diane everything. Convincing her to give Janie another chance.

Changing the world.

Or at least the world of The Manor.

"I've been thinking, Mother."

"About your lot in life?" Lady Diane asked. Haughty and disparaging.

"About Janie."

"The kitchen maid? She is no longer employed here."

"She —"

"She was found in a compromising position," Lady Diane interrupted, and walked quickly to her little writing desk in the corner of the room. It was by the windows, but didn't face them. Instead, it faced the great Tudor tapestry on the wall. As if Lady Diane wished only to see the world as others had made it, not the world as it was. "And she was found in possession of these."

She pulled a stack of papers from the drawer of the desk, turned, and held them up in one hand. Evidence. A flaming torch of condemnation.

Charlotte recognized them immediately.

"Those are mine," she whispered. But not loud enough for her mother to hear.

"Mrs. Griffiths thought they were evidence that the kitchen maid was trying to better herself. And writing scandalous lies about the people of this household." Lady Diane scanned one page after another.

Charlotte swallowed. Mrs. Griffiths thought they were Janie's. But didn't her mother recognize Charlotte's handwriting?

"A young girl in love with an Italian count," Lady Diane scoffed. "A count who looks remarkably like our second footman. And the lady of the house." She paused and Charlotte saw pain in her expression. "Not a very flattering portrait."

Lady Diane looked up and Charlotte could see that she knew. She knew her daughter wrote those pages. And she was waiting for Charlotte to deny it, so it could be blamed on someone else. Or to apologize.

But Charlotte found she could do neither.

"Those are mine," she said, more forcefully than before. Her mother waited, but Charlotte had nothing else to say. What she had written was the truth. At least now her mother knew how she felt.

"A warped sense of imagination," Lady Diane said, her voice as quiet as a curse. "We have been too lenient. Allowed you too much freedom. It leads to invention. To scandal. To writing this *trash*."

Charlotte could taste the charcoal of disgust in Lady Diane's voice.

"I'm going to burn these." Lady Diane strode to the fireplace, and Charlotte leapt to meet her, her hand outstretched. But the fire had not been lit, the heat of the summer overwhelming even within the cold stone walls of The Manor. They stopped in front of it, both of them dumbfounded.

"Why?" Charlotte looked up at her mother's hard face, the angles of the cheekbones and the aquiline nose. Lady Diane gripped the pages more tightly.

"Because I will not allow you to bring scandal upon this family."

"How is writing scandalous?" Charlotte asked. She felt small and frantic, like a tiny trapped animal.

"We did not raise you to be a writer," Lady Diane said. "We did not raise you to daydream about the footman. We raised you to be a daughter of this manor. To make an advantageous marriage. And to live by our rules."

Lady Diane dropped the sheaf of papers back into the drawer and slid another to the top of her desk. A letter, on The Manor's embossed paper.

"I will send you to finishing school," she said, signing it with a flourish.

"I won't go." Charlotte squared her shoulders.

"Yes, you will," Lady Diane said, her voice low and ominous. "You have no choice. Because you cannot survive in the outside world. But first, you will go back out to that party and dance with Andrew Broadhurst. You will act as if nothing has changed — because nothing has. And tomorrow, you will pack your bags."

Lady Diane strode from the room, leaving Charlotte alone with the spindly tables and the tapestries.

In the past, Charlotte would have cried in grief and frustration. Even a few days ago, she *would* have put on a meek smile and gone in search of Andrew.

Like a good girl.

As she stepped through the doorway, she saw Mr. Foyle, the butler, escort Lady Diane into the center of the hall and spin her regally into the dance. The first footman held a hand out to Lady Beatrice.

Charlotte walked across the marble hall to find Lawrence. And stepped into the circle of his arms.

She wanted to kiss him until her lips were numb. Lose herself in his smell of soap and silver.

But when they moved into the dance, Lawrence held her away from him. One hand clasped around hers, the other with its fingers barely touching her shoulder. It wasn't like the dance downstairs at all.

She didn't feel like Nellie Bly, or a character from a book. Not like Rosalind, the most courageous of Shakespeare's characters. She didn't even feel like mousy Jane Eyre, ready to profess her love to Rochester.

She felt like Charlotte Edmonds. Good girl. Cocooned in velvet and luxury. Swaddled. Bound in it. Unable to move or think or act for herself.

The music was suddenly too loud. The colors too vibrant. The spinning of the checkered floor made her feel dizzy and disoriented. The dance that she had so looked forward to was nothing like she expected.

"Lady Charlotte, are you all right?" Lawrence looked down at her.

He knew. He understood. He would help her escape.

"I have to leave," she said. Almost to herself.

*Tonight.*

She looked up at him. "Come with me," she whispered.

Lawrence looked surprised for an instant and then grinned, his deep-set eyes glinting. They were a beautiful blue, but there was something almost . . . dangerous about them.

"The doors are open," he said, his voice low and rumbling.

Lawrence guided her into the sitting room and through the French doors on the other side. The doors that looked out over the drive, the lawn, out to the gatehouse and the road that dipped down to Saints Hill and beyond.

Charlotte took a deep breath, glad to be away from the echoing marble. In this corner of the porch, she couldn't even hear the voices of the dancers.

When she turned, Lawrence put his arms around her and she was lost. In the gentleness of his touch on her face and throat. And in the heat of his mouth on hers.

But the kiss did nothing to quell her confusion. He no longer tasted of raspberries, but of port and cigars.

Charlotte started to pull away, to try to rediscover her emotions.

"Wait," Lawrence murmured, his lips running up her jaw. "Sarah."

Charlotte's heart stopped. Had he called her *Sarah*?

Charlotte turned to look at him, and Lawrence covered her mouth with his before she could speak.

And a voice from the doorway chased all thoughts from her mind.

"Well, here you are!"

Fran Caldwell stood silhouetted in the French doors, one hand on her hip, the other casually on the arm of Andrew Broadhurst. She strode across the paving stones, the beads in her hem glittering darkly.

Charlotte's heart thudded to a halt. A drenching like rain swept through her body from her toes to the top of her head. Elation. And agony. Courage. And self-recrimination.

*Oh my God, what have I done?*

She was saved. Andrew Broadhurst would never want her now.

And she was lost.

Charlotte felt her knees buckle. They actually started to crumple beneath her weight. And no one was there to catch her, so she steadied herself on the hard stone wall of The Manor.

Beside Charlotte, Lawrence froze. As if by his being as still as possible, no one would notice or see him. Charlotte thought for a second that maybe he would hold her hand. But maybe it was she who should claim their right to be together. Though when she reached her little finger out to his, Lawrence stepped away.

Distancing himself.

"Really, Charlotte," Fran drawled with false surprise. "A footman? You're as bad as the kitchen maid."

"I —" Charlotte hesitated. She was about to say she loved Lawrence. But did she?

She looked at Andrew, who still stood, unmoving, in the doorway, his face shrouded in shadows thrown by the blazing chandeliers behind him.

Fran leaned forward to whisper into Charlotte's ear. "What would your mother say?"

Fran drew back with a wicked smile on her lips. Charlotte knew exactly what her mother would say. And finishing school wouldn't be the worst of her threats.

So Charlotte turned and ran.

Down the stairs and onto the drive, looking for a place to hide. She hoped Lawrence would follow her, but he didn't.

She may have imagined him calling her name.

# Chapter 16

It was dark in the pantry. Just a crack of light at the bottom of the door. The room smelled of molasses and sugar, of bitter chocolate and cinnamon and flour. Of the sticky residue of strawberry jam. Of her mother. Of home.

Janie sat with her back up against the fifty-pound bag of flour, the floor slightly dusty beneath her fingers. Not dusty, floury. No matter how often she swept the pantry floor, it always seemed the flour got the better of her.

The door swung open a crack, letting in a pencil of light. Janie put her head down and covered it with her arms, elbows up around her ears. She didn't want to talk to anyone. Didn't want to see anyone.

"I thought you'd be in here."

The only voice that could make her cry. That could make her feel worse than she already did. Because she wanted more than anything for her mother to be proud of her.

The bag of flour shifted against Janie's back as Mrs. Seward leaned on it, as well.

"I always came here to cry, too," she said.

"I'm not crying." Janie pressed her forehead to her knees.

"Then you've got more strength than I ever did," Mrs. Seward said and sighed. "But then, I think I already knew that."

Janie didn't look up, but allowed her body to lean over and come to rest on her mother's. Comfort. Security. Just for a moment.

"I've got nothing, Ma," she said into her knees.

"Now, don't you say that, Janie Mae."

Janie lifted her head, the loose hairs from her braid trailing across her face. "I don't!" she said. "I don't have a job. Mrs. Griffiths sacked me with the blessing of Lady Diane herself. I've lost my friends." *Charlotte. Harry.* "And I'm going to lose you, too."

"You're never going to lose me, sweeting," her mother said. "I'm afraid you're stuck with me. And you can't lose your friends, either. Not if they're really your friends."

"I've said things . . ." The things she said to Charlotte. They didn't bear thinking about.

"So you apologize," Mrs. Seward said.

"And Harry hates me," Janie whispered.

"Harry Peasgood?" Her mother almost laughed. "Anyone can see that boy loves you more than life itself."

Janie's heart squeezed, as if it would stop beating altogether.

"He spread stories about me," she said, barely able to get the words past the lump in her throat. "Things he knew nothing about. Things that weren't even true."

"That doesn't sound like the Harry I know."

"I can't think who else it was."

"Secrets can't be kept forever," her mother said. "The tighter you hold them, the more they struggle out of your grasp."

"But none of it was a secret, Ma!" Janie moved away. "I never wrote those things. I never encouraged Lawrence."

"You never sneaked upstairs to play at being a lady's maid? You never fell in love with Harry Peasgood?"

Janie opened her mouth to say no. But found that she couldn't.

"No one knows the truth until it's told, Janie."

Janie's frustration built up again. "Like you've told it?" she asked. "You're leaving. Going to work for Lady Beatrice. I can understand you not wanting to tell Lady Diane, but why didn't you tell me?"

"Some truths are not ours to tell," Mrs. Seward said, her back straightening against the canvas flour sack. "And I'm not going to work for Lady Beatrice."

"So you're going to stay here?" *Without me?* Janie felt all of her optimism leave her. Her mother had given up a good position to stay at The Manor with her. And Janie had ruined that.

"Is that you, Miss Seward?"

The storeroom door cracked open, revealing a pair of black, shiny shoes and sharply creased trousers.

Mrs. Seward leapt up and started brushing the flour from her skirts.

"Lord Broadhurst," she said. "How can we help you?"

Janie stood more slowly, feeling disoriented. Guests never came downstairs. Certainly not earls-to-be.

"I'm afraid it's *Miss* Seward I'm looking for," Lord Broadhurst said with a little bow.

"I'm Janie," she corrected him. No one had called her anything else in her entire life. Unless you counted Charlotte and Miss Caldwell calling her *Jenny*.

Lord Broadhurst hesitated. “It’s my understanding that Lady Charlotte was training you to be a lady’s maid, so I thought Miss Seward was appropriate.”

“I’m training to be a cook, Lord Broadhurst,” Janie said with a glance at her mother. “So just Janie is fine for now.”

“I’m afraid I need your help, Janie,” Lord Broadhurst said in a rush. “You see, Lady Charlotte has gone missing.”

Janie’s head snapped up. “Missing?”

“Good,” Lord Broadhurst said, “I wasn’t wrong to come to you.”

“What does her mother say?” Mrs. Seward asked.

“I thought it best not to involve her mother at present,” Lord Broadhurst said with a cough. “Miss Caldwell and I may have seen Lady Charlotte in a rather . . . interesting predicament. Something she probably doesn’t want her mother to know about.”

*Then Miss Caldwell has probably told Lady Diane already,* Janie thought.

“Miss Caldwell recommended that I find you,” Lord Broadhurst added.

Janie felt as if the very foundation of her world had slipped.

“What happened?” she asked.

Lord Broadhurst took a deep breath and then steadied his gaze on her. His dark eyes were penetrating.

"She was outside the ball, on the porch." He cleared his throat. "With a footman."

*Oh, no.*

"Is she still with him?" Janie asked, her mind racing. Would they really run away together? Like in one of Charlotte's stories. So very romantic, but so very wrong.

"No."

Janie wasn't sure if she should be surprised or vexed on Charlotte's behalf. But looking into Lord Broadhurst's concerned face, she felt relief more than anything.

"Where do you think she went?"

"She ran. Along the drive and toward the kitchen courtyard. I thought she might have come in through the servants' entrance. The hall boy was kind enough to bring me through."

Harry.

"Where did he go?" Janie asked. Harry didn't want to see her. Couldn't stand to be around her.

"He's searching the basement. He said he knows all the good hiding places."

"You got the right man for the job, Lord Broadhurst," Janie said, pacing the hall. "Harry knows everything there is to know about The Manor."

"That's funny," Lord Broadhurst said, cocking his head to one side. "He said the same thing about you."

"Once we've searched the house, we'll have to think about the grounds," Janie said. Her fear of the walk to the icehouse in the dark loomed large, but she pushed it away.

"Is there anywhere she might have gone?" Lord Broadhurst asked. "I worry she may come to some harm."

"Or not return at all," Janie finished for him.

"Quite." Lord Broadhurst ran both hands roughly through his hair and looked at her pleadingly.

Janie stopped her pacing and closed her eyes. Trying to envision where Charlotte's imagination would take her. She thought back through all the places she'd seen her in the past week. Her room. The kitchen. The garden.

The lake.

"I think I know where she is," Janie said, heading for the courtyard. She didn't care that she brushed Lord Broadhurst aside in her haste. She didn't care for precedence or class. She cared only for Charlotte.

# Chapter 17

It was bloody cold in the woods. And dark.

Charlotte regretted her impetuous flight as soon as the canopy of leaves blocked out the moonlight. The shadowy wood held none of the heat of the day. Her flimsy gown did nothing to fend off the chill.

Fingers of dry bracken tugged at the chiffon of her hem, and she felt every rock and tree root beneath her slippers. She had somehow wandered off the path and lost her sense of direction. She wasn't convinced she would be able to find the lake at all, given her disorientation.

What she wouldn't give for Janie's sensible shoes. And her company.

Charlotte stopped walking and reassessed her situation. She was being sent to finishing school. Her mother was going to find a way to stop her from writing. One so-called friend — Fran — was about to go and tell the entire world that Charlotte had been kissing a footman, bringing scandal to the family and ruining her reputation. Her other friend — Janie — didn't even see her as a friend, and after all the things Charlotte had said, she couldn't blame her.

And as Charlotte stood there, unable to choose whether to go forward or go back, she had to admit to herself that Andrew Broadhurst wasn't the ogre she'd imagined he was. Now she had ruined any possibility of getting to know him better.

Not only that, but Lawrence hadn't followed her. He hadn't grabbed her hand and run down the drive with her, ready to face the world at her side.

He had let her go.

A noise like a scream came from the trees, and Charlotte nearly screamed herself. Suddenly, a great shape swept over her — gray and gold and a glimmer of white. Silently, the owl soared between the trees and out into where she could see the glimmer of stars and a trace of moonlight.

It had shown her the way to the lake.

Charlotte used that as proof that forward was the way to go. Not back.

She couldn't go back.

Her mother just wanted her to disappear. The sixth child. The daughter. The extra.

The mistake.

Charlotte stumbled the rest of the way down to the water. The path was too dry to leave footprints, but the lakeshore was still damp, and her feet sank into the mud when she reached the water.

Good. Evidence that she had been there.

She wondered if anyone was out searching for her yet. Had Fran told just her mother? Or the entire assembly?

And would anyone care? Would her mother just think she had gone off in a sulk and not realize she was missing until morning? Would Sarah say anything when she went upstairs to help Charlotte change for bed?

Would Sarah even go, considering Charlotte had been caught kissing the very footman Sarah had her sights on?

"No use feeling sorry for yourself," Charlotte said out loud, sitting down on the rock to remove her slippers.

She sat, muddy shoes in her hand, and smiled. Because she *could* feel sorry for herself. The scandal. The servants not wanting to be associated with her. Lady Diane's censure.

But she didn't.

Charlotte felt — for the first time in her life — free.

Drawing her right hand back, she threw one slipper as far out into the lake as she could. The splash sounded loud against the backdrop of the trees, the ripples silvering in the moonlight.

"I've taken control of my own destiny," she said, hauling back and throwing the other shoe. "I'm writing my own story."

Charlotte pulled off her stockings and flung them for luck, but they fluttered like cobwebs and settled wetly on the lake surface not a yard from her feet. Ignoring them, she stood, her toes squelching in the mud on the lakeshore, planning her next move.

She took a step. And another. The lake lapping at her ankles. Soaking up into the hem of her Worth gown.

"Janie!"

She thought she heard Harry calling out. A trick of her overactive imagination. Janie had been fired. Harry, too, probably. And some of it was her fault.

They'd be better off without her.

"Charlotte?"

The voice was so close Charlotte almost lost her balance on the shifty bottom of the lake. She turned to see Janie just at the edge of the trees. She was perched on the balls of her feet, one hand on a tree for balance.

"What are you doing?" Janie asked, her head cocked to one side.

"Leaving."

Janie sucked in a breath. "Why?"

"Because Mother wants to send me off to finishing school. In Yorkshire. With a bunch of insipid girls whose only goal is to be a good hostess and marry well. Where the only books are *Aesop's Fables* and Mrs. Beeton."

Janie's mouth quirked up on one side. "Mrs. Beeton has some good advice," she said. "She at least knows how to sew on a button."

"I think I'd rather stay here."

Charlotte heard an indistinct splash, and a shiver ran up the back of her leg. She wondered what lived in the lake.

"You've never wanted to stay here. You've always wanted to see the rest of the world."

Charlotte snorted. "Yorkshire is not the rest of the world."

The water around her calves shifted, and Janie's eyes left her. Suddenly, Charlotte knew that someone else was behind her. Probably Harry. She'd heard him calling. She cursed herself for not realizing that Janie was trying to distract her. Trying to delay her. This wasn't what she had imagined at all.

Without thinking, she took another step into the lake, but the ground fell away beneath her and she plunged into the cold, inky blackness, the shock making her gasp water right into her lungs.

An arm came around her waist, and another across her chest, and she was wrenched back into the air, coughing and spluttering.

And kicking.

But the arms didn't let go.

Janie rushed into the lake, and Harry burst out of the trees behind her, racing to reach her before she, too, fell off the ledge.

And Charlotte squirmed far enough around to look up into the dependable brown eyes of Andrew Broadhurst.

"Yorkshire isn't the end of the world, either," he whispered.

But he didn't let her go.

Janie wrestled out of Harry's grip and splashed toward them.

"What were you thinking?" Janie shouted, and looked like she was about to wrench Charlotte right out of Andrew's arms and throw her back into the lake. But Andrew held out a hand to steady her, and then lifted Charlotte out of the water and carried her to shore.

As soon as he set Charlotte down, Janie put a hand on both of her shoulders and shook her roughly.

"How could you be so stupid?" she asked, and then wrapped both arms around Charlotte in the tightest hug she'd ever received in her life.

Throughout it all, Andrew Broadhurst never let go of her hand.

Janie pulled back and gazed at Charlotte, tears streaming down her face.

"Janie?" Charlotte said, feeling panicky. "You never cry."

"I thought you were going to do something stupid," Janie said, taking a deep breath. She looked down at the muddy bank, and then used the tips of her fingers to wipe below her eyes.

Charlotte frowned. "What did you think I was going to do?"

"Charlotte, I read that story," Janie said, pressing her lips together and looking her in the eye. "Your story. About the girl who falls in love with the Italian count. How she goes down to the lake —"

"Lake Como," Charlotte added.

"And throws herself in." Janie hugged Charlotte again. "It's not worth it. This isn't some Gothic novel, this is real life."

"Janie." Charlotte couldn't keep the shock from her voice. "You read my story?"

"It was your writing. It wasn't my business to be reading any of it. And I only read the first page. I was sorry at the time, but I'm not now. It's the only reason I knew where to find you."

Charlotte laughed a little, but felt a stinging in her eyes. "If you'd read more, you would have known it was a ruse. She was *pretending* to kill herself. So she could escape."

Janie stepped back, nearly toppling over.

"So that's what you were planning?" she asked in a whisper. "To disappear?"

Charlotte nodded. But as she did so, she began to see the foolishness of her actions. "I thought if people saw my footprints here, and found my slippers and stockings floating in the lake, they'd just assume . . ."

Everyone was staring at her.

"I imagined no one would look for me. That I could escape. That I would be . . . free."

"You'll never be free, Charlotte," Janie said.

Charlotte felt it like a blow. Janie the risk taker. Janie her friend. Telling her she was stuck in this life forever. She sagged backward, and Andrew caught her again.

"She means you'll never be able to escape the people who care about you," he murmured into her ear.

Charlotte shivered and he let her go, taking off his dinner jacket to wrap around her shoulders.

"We would *always* come looking for you," Janie added. "I think your imagination got away with you. You probably had the whole script written out in your head. You'd come down to the lake, leave your clues, and disappear. Your mother would host a society funeral, bemoaning the fact that she hadn't gotten to know you sooner."

Charlotte felt a stab of truth. Her mother would care more about the funeral than her disappearing daughter.

"But you know, Charlotte," Janie said quietly, "you can't always write the book of your life. Things happen that you don't plan."

Charlotte smiled weakly. "People are unpredictable," she said. "They never do in real life what I think they'll do in my head." Looking at Janie, Charlotte thought maybe that was a good thing.

Janie laughed. "Isn't that the truth?" Charlotte saw her cast a sideways look at Harry.

Charlotte sighed. "I thought I saw things so clearly. That people are the characters I write down. But no one is. Nothing is like I imagined it."

"That can be a good thing," Janie said. She widened her eyes a bit, her mouth curving upward at the edges, and then flicked a glance over Charlotte's shoulder.

Charlotte knew exactly what she meant. Andrew Broadhurst. He wasn't at all as she'd imagined. He'd seen her kissing someone else. And yet, he'd come out into the wood to find her.

And Lawrence hadn't.

Charlotte took a deep breath. "I'm sorry," she said. She forced herself to look Janie in the eye, rather than hanging her head in regret. "I'm sorry for all those things I said to you. And I'm sorry things are what they are, that my father is the lord of The Manor and you're its kitchen maid."

"Not anymore," Janie said wryly.

"And I'm so sorry for that, too," Charlotte added, nearly in tears. "For my mother and her rules."

"It's not her fault they were broken."

"No, it's mine," Harry said. Charlotte noticed that Janie wouldn't look at him. "But I didn't tell anyone about your writing, Lady Charlotte. I saw Janie hide it, but I never saw it again."

"Then who did tell?" Janie spun on him.

Harry shrugged helplessly. "All I know is it wasn't me, Janie. I'd never do anything to hurt you."

Charlotte could see that clearly. She just hoped Janie could, too. A breeze came in off the lake, stirring the wet hair on her neck, and she shivered again.

"We should go back to The Manor." Andrew put a hand on her shoulder. "They'll be getting worried about you."

Charlotte suppressed her snort of disbelief. Instead, she just nodded and took a step forward. A sharp stone lacerated her instep and she cringed.

"My shoes," she said. "They're in the lake."

Suddenly, Janie laughed. "How did you think you were going to run away with no shoes and wearing a wet and ruined Worth gown?"

"I guess I didn't plan that far," Charlotte said, laughing at herself.

"Take mine," Janie said, bending down to unlace her shoes. "I dare say my feet are tougher than yours."

"No, Janie," Charlotte said, stopping her. "I dare say I'm the one who can afford to put her feet up all day after cutting them to ribbons through my own stupidity. You don't have that luxury."

Janie started to argue, and Charlotte prepared a rebuttal, but Andrew interrupted.

"Before we prove how selfless you both are, let me offer

an alternative." He turned to Charlotte and held out a hand. "If you will allow me?"

He put her right arm around his neck, bent, and lifted her up into his arms, the scent of sandalwood and spice surrounding her. She looked up into his dark eyes and wondered how she ever could have thought he was boring.

"Thank you," she whispered.

"It's my pleasure," he murmured. "I had hoped to hold you in my arms at some point this evening. And this is better than the hesitation waltz."

The chill in Charlotte's chest became a starburst as she felt the flush rise from breastbone to forehead. A flush not of embarrassment, she discovered, but of pleasure. She buried her face in his neck — in his scent — and let the present happen. Without imagining it to be different, or wondering what would happen next.

# Chapter 18

Janie slowed and stood on the edge of the drive. She watched as Lord Broadhurst carried Charlotte right to the front steps of The Manor and set her down gently.

As servants, she and Harry weren't allowed in the front entrance. As an ex-servant, she wasn't even sure she'd be allowed in the kitchen courtyard. And she didn't want to face it all anyway — Tess's jealousy and Sarah's spite. Mollie's vacillating loyalties.

"I understand why Charlotte wanted to disappear," she said.

"You're talking to me."

Janie turned to Harry. The light from the windows of The Manor streaked across his face. He wore an expression of wary hope.

"I just don't understand why you told on me," she murmured.

"I didn't, Janie. Can't you understand that? Yes, I thought the writing was yours, but I never told anyone about it. It was obviously private."

Janie felt a pang of guilt. She knew it was private and yet she'd read some.

"But someone told about . . ." Janie could hardly say it. She didn't even want to admit to it. Not with Harry standing right in front of her. Listening. "About me and Lawrence."

"That wasn't me, either." Sadness came off Harry in waves.

"I didn't kiss him," Janie said quickly. "I couldn't. I knew it could cost me my job."

"But you wanted to."

Janie nodded, unable to look at him. "For a moment."

The truth felt like a sliver of ice in her heart.

"Even if I had seen it," Harry said, "I would never have said a word. I know this is your home."

"If there's one thing I learned tonight, it's that I had a blinkered vision of home," she said. "I thought it was the trees and the Weald and the lake. I thought it was the kitchen. But Charlotte belongs here even more than I do, and she never felt at home."

Janie studied Harry's face. The splash of freckles across his nose, the curls that never seemed tame. His eyes like something rich and intoxicating. Like champagne.

"I think, maybe, home is being with people who love you," she finished.

Harry nodded, slowly. He seemed afraid to speak. Afraid of *her*, and her false accusations. A knot of shame rose in the back of her throat.

"I always had people who loved me," she continued, speaking around it. "My aunt and my cousins did in their own way, I suppose. But they never had time for me. All their time was spent on subsistence. Only when I came here did I know what it was like to be loved. No, to be cherished. To love without need or dependence, but with simple generosity. I never want to lose that."

"But your mother is leaving."

Janie took a deep breath.

"I wasn't talking about my mother."

Harry stiffened visibly. It was so quiet in the courtyard, she heard him swallow.

Finally, she worked up the courage to reach out to him. To place her hand on his cheek and take one step closer.

"I was talking about you," she whispered.

Emotions unfurled across Harry's face. Joy. Fear. Awakening. Disbelief.

Janie pulled him closer. She closed the gap between them, raised her face, and pressed her mouth to his. When his lips parted in surprise, she pressed harder, afraid of losing him. Of scaring him away.

But he wrapped his arms around her, pulling her so close she could feel the racing of his heart against hers.

Janie moved her head, so her lips were at his ear.

"I never want to leave you."

Harry's grip relaxed and he stepped away, taking her face in his hands. Silently, he studied her, his eyes searching her face. And then he kissed her, his lips soft and knowing and perfectly matched to hers. In that instant, Janie felt like nothing could separate them.

Until a shout from the front entrance caused them to spring apart, straightening clothes and avoiding eye contact. Janie knew it was a sure sign of guilt, but she couldn't help it. Without Harry, her hands felt idle.

"How dare you?"

Lady Diane's voice carried clearly across the drive, ringing in the moonlight.

Janie looked at Harry guiltily, and then up at the house.

She could see Lady Diane in the French doorway of the sitting room. But she wasn't facing the drive. She wasn't berating Janie and Harry. She was talking to someone inside.

"Who do you think you are?"

"Charlotte," Janie said, and started toward the house.

"We can't go in that way." Harry grabbed her hand, but she shook him off.

"I have to get to her. I have to let her know she's not alone."

"And if we walk right up into the sitting room, we'll never work again."

Janie hesitated and then shook her head. "It doesn't matter."

"It *does* matter," Harry said, and physically blocked her way. "I won't let you. But I know every inch of every passageway. I'll get you there."

# Chapter 19

Before Charlotte reentered The Manor, she glanced back to see Janie and Harry hesitating at the edge of the lawn. She wanted to grab Janie's hand and bring her up the stone stairs and through the marble hall.

But she needed to do this on her own.

Or perhaps with Andrew Broadhurst behind her. It turned out it was good to have someone dependable at your back.

As she climbed the great stairs to The Manor's main entrance, her gown left a damp trail behind her. The stone felt cold and slick beneath her bare feet, and her hair clung wetly to her neck and temples.

"I must look a fright," she murmured. She imagined appearing in the doorway like a half-drowned cat, swept away by the full flood of her mother's wrath.

Her hands fluttered at her sides, and Andrew stepped forward and grabbed one. His hand felt so warm. So real.

When she stepped into the great marble hall, everything stopped. The guests were buttoned up in coats and had their hats on. The musicians were packing. Her mother was nowhere to be seen.

"Is it over?" Charlotte asked. A ball — even a servants' ball — could go on into the wee hours. She couldn't have been gone that long.

For a moment, no one said a word. Then Fran appeared at the top of the grand staircase and ran down it, calling, "She's not in her room, and I've checked all the others."

She stopped when she caught sight of Charlotte in the doorway and then ran at her.

"Charlotte!" she cried, throwing her arms around her. "You're back!"

"I'm wet," Charlotte said, confused. She tried to extract herself from Fran's grip, regretting having to let go of Andrew's hand in the process.

"I don't care," Fran sobbed, clinging more tightly. "I'm sorry!"

The rest of the guests suddenly came to life, murmuring and nodding and hustling to the door or up the stairs to their rooms like rats from a sinking ship. Charlotte couldn't believe she'd caused this much concern.

"Where's Mother?" she asked.

Fran stiffened and then pulled away. "Lady Diane is in the sitting room," she said.

Charlotte took a deep breath and walked to the sitting room's door. Her mother stood by the French entrance, but didn't look out. Her eyes were on her sister by the fireplace.

"Mother?" Charlotte said and both women turned to her. Relief flooded Aunt Beatrice's face, but Lady Diane went pale with anger.

Charlotte could feel Andrew behind her. He wasn't close enough to touch, but he was there. Uncowed by her mother's fury. By the white knuckles of her hand on the edge of the table. By the eyes staring daggers at him, obviously waiting for him to excuse himself graciously.

But Andrew Broadhurst didn't move. When Charlotte glanced back, he had schooled his face into a mask of unaffected placidity and was standing his ground.

"Where is he?" Lady Diane asked, her voice a low growl.

Charlotte froze. Fran had shown more concern than this. The guests in their top hats and summer coats had been more relieved to see her safe.

"Who?"

Lady Diane became very still. "The *footman*."

"I don't know."

Lady Diane narrowed her eyes. "You weren't running off with him?"

Charlotte had imagined just that scenario. The first time Lawrence kissed her. When she wrote the story of the Italian count. When she stumbled into the darkness of the forest. She could still picture it — the two of them overlooking the Côte d'Azur. But the picture was fading.

"No, Mother."

"You were going *alone*?" Lady Diane made this sound worse than running off with a footman. "Where on earth did you think you were going?"

Charlotte lifted her chin.

But her mother didn't wait for a reply.

"You have *ruined* that gown." Lady Diane shook her head. "And your shoes . . ."

Charlotte wiggled her toes, realizing she hadn't gone barefoot in the house since she was very young.

It felt . . . liberating.

Lady Diane obviously saw the action as subversive.

"I will not speak with you," she said. "Get out. Now."

Any self-respecting daughter of The Manor should have lowered her eyes and trudged upstairs without another word. But Charlotte had more to say.

"No." With that one word, all the strength went out of Charlotte's limbs and she felt as if her very skin was lifting away. She had never defied her mother.

"How dare you?" Lady Diane cried, her fury surpassing her desire to maintain her flawless façade.

"I need you to see me," Charlotte said, controlling her voice more than she could control the icy wash that ran from her head to her toes and back again. "I am a person, Mother. Not just a burden."

"Don't be ridiculous," Lady Diane hissed.

"Let her speak," Aunt Beatrice said, and in her aunt's eyes, Charlotte could see acceptance. Encouragement.

"Who do you think you are?" Lady Diane turned on her sister.

"This isn't about Aunt Beatrice," Charlotte said firmly. "This is about me. About the way you treat me. Like I have no self. Like I have no voice."

"I've given you everything," Lady Diane said.

"You've given me dresses and nurses and governesses. You've given me servants to feed me and clothe me. You've given me books. And for all those things, I thank you. But you haven't given me love."

"What do you know?" Lady Diane snapped.

Charlotte knew that she always felt small and inconsequential. That her worth was measured by her marriageability.

"I know that if you loved me, you would let me make my own choices." Saying the words was as liberating as wiggling her bare toes. But the truth behind them left a bitter aftertaste.

"And if your choices lead you to kissing a footman and running away to God knows where to get yourself soaked in the middle of the night? You expect me to let you do those things?" Lady Diane demanded.

"I expect you to let me make mistakes!" Charlotte cried. "I expect you to give me guidance, not censure. I don't want to do everything you say. Be everything you want me to be. I want to be my own self. Make my own choices. I want to fall in love, not marry someone because you tell me to."

"Hear, hear."

She felt Andrew's murmur more than heard it. And the subsequent rush of embarrassment was followed by a rush of warmth.

"I don't think we can choose who we love," Charlotte

said slowly, looking her mother in the eye, "or have it forced upon us."

"You choose with whom you associate. Love is a fabrication. An invention. The stuff of fiction and overheated imagination."

Charlotte felt desperation rising like welts on her skin. Were her emotions just another component of her fevered imaginings? Was love just a fairy story?

"So you see, Charlotte." Lady Diane's tone was condescending. Like she knew she had the upper hand. "It's impossible to love someone with whom you don't associate. Therefore you cannot possibly love a servant."

Across the room, at the little door that opened into the space beneath the grand staircase, Charlotte saw Janie and Harry.

Holding hands. *That* was love. That was real.

Lady Diane didn't see them. Her penetrating gaze never left Charlotte's face.

"Oh, I can love a 'servant,' Mother," Charlotte said, feeling a surge of courage stiffen her resolve. "I've loved Janie like a sister for a while. Because she accepts me for who I am. Because she treats me like I'm visible. I couldn't love her less because she's a kitchen maid. Love is worth the risk."

Lady Diane's gaze flicked from one of Charlotte's eyes to the other, as if she could see the meaning there behind Charlotte's words. She glanced once at Aunt Beatrice and then turned back to Charlotte, looking almost bewildered.

"I feel like I don't even know you anymore," Lady Diane sighed.

Charlotte knew she was expected to feel guilty. But she could no longer live up to her mother's expectations. "I don't think you ever knew me."

Lady Diane flinched as if she had been struck. Her eyes clouded and she blinked them rapidly before shaking her head and gathering her skirts.

"I no longer wish to hear any of this," she said, moving toward the door. Her words tumbled over each other in her haste to get them out and get away. "You're just like your mother."

"What do you mean?" Charlotte asked, scrambling to understand. "I'm nothing like you."

Lady Diane stopped abruptly, as if she had hit a wall. She clenched her fists.

"Nothing," she said. But she didn't leave.

Charlotte looked around the room. Janie and Harry looked as perplexed as she felt. Aunt Beatrice was staring at her sister with a mixture of shock and fascination.

“I think —” Aunt Beatrice began, but Lady Diane spun around and silenced her with a hiss.

“You have no right to think.”

Aunt Beatrice straightened her spine. “I have every right to speak my mind. You have no control over me.”

“Neither does any sense of responsibility. Or family honor. Or morality.” Lady Diane advanced on her sister surely and deliberately with every word, the timbre of her voice deepening with threat.

Andrew put a hand on Charlotte’s shoulder. She stepped back and took his other hand in hers.

“We should go,” she said, her voice quiet and unsure.

“No!” Lady Beatrice took a step forward, but her sister blocked her.

Lady Diane’s face was white and rigid with fury, the lines around her mouth and eyes deeply creased.

But Beatrice stood her ground. “Isn’t it time I told the truth?”

“No,” Lady Diane said quietly, her voice as steely as her gaze. “It’s time *I* told the truth.”

She turned to Charlotte, her features softening a little, but her voice took on a sharper edge. “You say I haven’t loved you? You say that choosing with whom you associate is worth the risk?”

Lady Diane glanced once at Aunt Beatrice and then back at Charlotte.

"Your *aunt* once had a dalliance like yours. With a member of the staff." Lady Diane pressed her lips together. "With the *coachman*."

Charlotte found it difficult to swallow around the lump in her throat. She felt Andrew shift his weight, and she suddenly feared he would walk away. But he moved to stand so close to her she could feel the warmth of his body through the jacket she still wore.

"She said it was love." Each word Lady Diane spoke was as hard as granite.

"It was," Aunt Beatrice said.

Lady Diane flung out a hand to silence her. "Not only was the man a servant, he was married."

Charlotte looked at Beatrice, and it was like watching her heart break.

"When she became pregnant, she came to me. Crying. She had ruined herself. She would ruin the family. I told her she would never marry. That no one would ever want her. That if our parents were alive, they'd disown her. That I would send her away and never see her again."

Beatrice wouldn't look at any of them anymore. She stood with her head down and her hands clasped before her as if in supplication. As if she had suddenly become the girl in her sister's memory.

"In the end, none of those things came true," Lady Diane continued. "I made sure no one knew about her. I claimed the pregnancy as my own. My husband had a doctor order bed rest for me. I didn't attend the Season. I didn't throw any parties. I didn't see any of my friends."

Lady Diane paused and cast a venomous look at her sister. But that look lost its potency with her next words.

"For her."

Lady Diane turned back to Charlotte. It seemed, to Charlotte, that her mother had lost some of her potency herself. That she was smaller. Frailer.

"I raised her baby as if she were my own," Lady Diane finished. "*That's* what love is."

Charlotte felt the weight of those words press the air from her lungs. She stared, unseeing, at the tapestry on the far side of the room, the strands of color blurry. Her vision faded around the edges. She felt nothing. Not the heat still trapped in the house. Not her wet gown clinging to her.

Not even her own heart.

"What are you saying?" she whispered. Her tongue felt thick, as if she could only form the words through great exertion.

The room rushed back into acute focus. The burgundy and black of her mother's dress. The mud on the hem of Janie's dress. The hazel of Beatrice's eyes.

So much like her own.

Lady Diane looked at Charlotte. No, she looked *behind* Charlotte. Her color didn't come back, but her strength seemed to. She tilted her head to one side and smiled graciously, as if she were speaking about the weather.

"You see, Lord Broadhurst," she said. "All is not as it seems at The Manor."

And then she collapsed.

# Chapter 20

Janie had spent her entire life making things appear other than they really were. Making meals appear effortless. Making herself appear invisible to the family of The Manor, as a good servant should. Trying to appear as if she wasn't terrified the world would change in an instant and the whole façade come crashing down around her.

She was shocked to discover that Lady Diane was the same. When the mistress of The Manor pitched over, Janie turned to Harry behind her. "Run for the doctor," she said.

Lady Beatrice ran to her sister, so Janie went to Charlotte, who stood like an effigy just inside the doorway to the marble hall. Staring at the crumpled figure on the floor. Lord Broadhurst stood right behind her, one hand on her shoulder.

"Harry's gone for the doctor," Janie told him, and then said to Charlotte, "Your mother will be all right."

"She's not my mother." Charlotte's voice was completely flat.

Lady Beatrice looked up, but Charlotte turned away. Janie didn't want to see the pain in Lady Beatrice's eyes. She wanted to rail at her for giving up her daughter. For coming back into her life now.

For running to her sister first.

But Janie didn't. Instead, she spoke to Lord Broadhurst. "I'll take Charlotte upstairs and send for a maid."

Janie put an arm around Charlotte's shoulder, still covered by Lord Broadhurst's dinner jacket.

The guests had scattered, leaving the marble hall empty and echoing. Janie wondered how much they had heard. She wondered how many of the neighbors would already be gossiping, how quickly the houseguests would depart in the morning.

She wondered if it mattered. The Edmonds family would not be able to escape the social repercussions triggered by the night's events.

For the first time in her life, Janie walked up the grand staircase of The Manor, Charlotte stumbling along with her. She guided Charlotte down the hall, past the painting of a high-masted ship almost toppling into the raging ocean, past Charles I still gazing at his queen. She pushed open the bedroom door and led Charlotte to an overstuffed chair.

"I'll ruin the upholstery," Charlotte muttered.

"I should think that's the least of your worries," Janie said, pulling the bell.

Charlotte's head jerked up. "Don't leave me," she said.

"Don't be daft. I'm not leaving you."

"You rang for Sarah."

"I rang for tea," Janie said and turned to look at Charlotte, small and bedraggled as she was. "You look like you could use it."

Charlotte slumped to the floor and pressed her forehead into the thick carpet.

"I don't even know who I am anymore," she said, her words muffled by the thick pile.

"You're you." Janie sat on the floor beside her and stroked her hair, carefully untangling the intricately pinned coils that had been knotted and saturated by lake water.

"Everything I thought was real was just imaginary," Charlotte said, turning her head just slightly. "Pretend."

"I'm sorry." Words didn't seem like enough. Even tears weren't enough. Charlotte's entire existence had been washed away in a single evening.

“How *could* she?” Charlotte cried, pressing the heels of her hands to her eyes. “With a servant?”

Janie stopped untangling Charlotte’s hair. “You said love is always worth the risk.”

Charlotte went rigid. “It is,” she whispered into her hands. “I meant what I said.”

“I know,” Janie said, hoping that she did. “Lawrence deserves a good punching for disappearing like that.”

“I didn’t mean him,” Charlotte said, sitting up. “I meant what I said about you. I need my friends right now, Janie. I need *you.* My mother is a stranger. I never even knew my father!”

“Lady Diane said he was Lady Beatrice’s coachman.”

“But she used to live here,” Charlotte said. “Lady Beatrice lived here until she married.”

Janie sat very still for a moment. She studied Charlotte’s eyes. Hazel. Like Beatrice’s.

Janie swallowed. “He was The Manor’s coachman?”

“He must have been,” Charlotte said, frowning. “But that was years ago. We’ve had a chauffeur for two years. And I don’t remember the coachman from when I was a child.”

“He would have been dismissed,” Janie said. Icy tendrils started wrapping themselves around her heart. “As soon as Lady Diane found out.”

"Well, *that's* true," Charlotte said bitterly. "Without a reference."

Janie nodded. "He would have left. Taken his wife with him."

Charlotte looked at her. "That's right. Mother — Lady Diane — said he was married."

"He would never have found another job in service," Janie whispered. She couldn't look Charlotte in the eye. Couldn't form the thoughts. It was as if the words formed themselves. "Maybe he joined the Army."

Charlotte may have whimpered. But Janie wasn't finished.

"He would have left his wife. Let her fend for herself. After all, she wasn't the one who had committed the indiscretion. She could still find work. She was employable. What he didn't think about was his baby." Janie finally dragged her gaze to meet Charlotte's. "His babies. He had two daughters. He never gave either one of them another thought."

Charlotte didn't breathe, just stared at her until Janie became so uncomfortable she almost stood up. She almost left the room. The Manor.

Charlotte blinked. "Are you telling me that your father —"

"Used to be the coachman," Janie finished for her. "He worked here for fifteen years. I was always told he got fired because of me. Because The Manor didn't want to support his baby."

Charlotte made a sound that could have been a laugh. "When really, it was supporting a different one."

For a long moment, they just looked at each other. Janie searched Charlotte's face for something familiar. She saw it in the arch of an eyebrow. The slight uplift at the end of the nose. The hint of red in the deep brown hair.

"I never knew my father, either," Janie said, her words sounding as if they had traveled a long distance over a broken road. "But I think I know my sister."

Janie waited, her heartbeat throbbing percussively at her temples. Her mind kept spinning, snagging on questions and broken images. She wished she had something to do with her hands — stirring or kneading or scrubbing — so she could slow her thoughts down and unpick the tangles.

Charlotte went completely still, staring. "Sister?" she whispered.

Then with a squeak, she threw her arms around Janie, almost knocking her back onto the floor.

Janie gasped in surprise and hugged Charlotte back. It felt strange, even after all they'd been through. The ghost of the invisible wall between upstairs and downstairs was still there.

"I'm so glad!" Charlotte said, hugging Janie more tightly. "I'm so glad I have a sister."

"I am, too," Janie said. Glad to have a sister, but so sad for her mother and father, and for Lady Beatrice. For all the consequences of their actions.

Then Charlotte laughed. Or perhaps she sobbed. It turned into a coughing fit that wracked her frame, and still she didn't let go.

Janie pulled away.

"I won't have a sister for long if you die of pneumonia from your trip into the lake," she said brusquely. "You need to change."

Charlotte stood up and shed the Worth gown, the chiffon puddling on the carpet, the dye already starting to streak. Janie shook it out and hung it up carefully.

"So do you," Charlotte said, shivering in her linen shift and corset. She pointed accusingly at Janie's sodden hem and squelching shoes.

"I'll go up in a minute," Janie said.

"You will not," Charlotte said, going to the wardrobe and pulling out a pretty, rose-colored tea gown. She held it up to Janie. "This should fit you, and you won't need a corset."

Janie stood, holding the dress at arm's length. "I can't wear this."

"It will fit you," Charlotte said, pulling out a similar gown in a pale blue.

"It's too nice." Janie started to hang it up again, but Charlotte stopped her.

"Wear it," she said solemnly and moved behind the bed and its velvet curtains to change.

Janie pulled off the cotton dress and slipped into the gown. It felt like summer against her skin. The hem was perhaps a little long; she could feel it tickling her toes. But Charlotte was right. It fit.

Janie turned to thank her, but Charlotte was almost buried headfirst in her cedar chest, rummaging around the bottom of it. She came up with two pairs of thick woolen socks and threw one at Janie.

"These will keep your feet warm," she said. "I stole them from my brother when he came home from Oxford one year." She paused and frowned. "My cousin, I guess. Not my brother."

"It will take some getting used to," Janie said.

They watched each other for a long moment more.

A knock at the door startled them and they both looked up.

"Come in?" Charlotte said, her voice tentative.

It could be anyone. Sarah. Mrs. Griffiths. Lady Diane.

Though Lady Diane didn't strike Janie as the sort of person who would knock before entering her daughter's room.

No one entered. Silence reigned on the other side of the door.

Janie looked at Charlotte, who stared at her, wide-eyed. So Janie crossed the room and carefully opened the door, peering around it to see who was there.

Lord Broadhurst stood in the hall, carrying a tray laden with a teapot, a cup and saucer, and a plate filled with tiny slices of cake.

"Miss Seward," he said, relief written all over his face. "I thought perhaps tea was in order."

He glanced at Charlotte and then back to Janie, his eyes full of sympathy.

"I rang for Sarah," Janie said, opening the door wider to allow him in, but he didn't move.

"I'm afraid the housemaid . . ." Lord Broadhurst paused. "The housemaid refused to answer Lady Charlotte's bell."

Janie turned just in time to see Charlotte's head sink to her knees again.

"The minx," Janie muttered under her breath and then looked up into the earl-to-be's startled face. "My apologies for my unguarded tongue, Lord Broadhurst."

"No apologies necessary," he said. "You expressed my thoughts admirably, and perhaps with more discretion."

He smiled, his eyes dancing. No wonder Charlotte appeared to like him now.

"Please come in," Charlotte said.

"I'm afraid it's not fitting for a single man to enter a maiden's bedchamber," Lord Broadhurst said, handing over the tray to Janie. "I just wanted to bring this."

"Oh, heavens," Charlotte said, standing up. "I think my reputation can take a bit more of a beating."

"I wouldn't add to your troubles, Charlotte." The way he said Charlotte's name made Janie want to cry. So much tenderness.

They stood there for a moment, the three of them, caught in a web of propriety. Janie wished they lived in a simpler world. She set the tea tray down on Charlotte's dressing table.

Lord Broadhurst seemed to collect himself. "And I only brought one cup. I do apologize, Miss Seward."

"Please, call me Janie," she said, easing past him. "And I can get my own. . . ."

The hidden door at the end of the hall opened, and Harry's face appeared around the jamb.

"Oh, Janie, everything's gone to . . ." He spotted Lord

Broadhurst and Charlotte through the doorway. ". . . gone to the dogs downstairs."

"Is Lady Diane all right?" Janie asked.

"The doctor's here," Harry said, walking silently up the hall. "He came right away."

"I should go to my mother," Charlotte said. She sounded weak and unsure.

"Her . . ." Harry hesitated. "Her sister is with her."

They were all silent for a moment, and Janie imagined she was not the only one trying to untangle which woman was mother and which sister.

Harry took a deep breath and added, "She said she didn't want to see you."

Charlotte bit her lip and turned her head away, the loose strands of hair covering her face.

"She never wanted me," she said. Lord Broadhurst laid a hand on her shoulder, and Charlotte shuddered. Janie's heart broke for her.

Harry shook his head and stepped closer. "Lady Diane, I mean," he said quickly. "Lady Beatrice . . . she said she'll come and find you. That you have a lot to talk about."

Charlotte blew air out through her nose in a sound that could have been a snort and could have been a sob. "That's an understatement," she said. Janie had to smile. If Charlotte could joke, she would be all right.

And Lord Broadhurst's hand hadn't moved from her shoulder.

"I'm going downstairs," Janie said. "Can I bring you anything else, Charlotte?"

Charlotte looked evenly at Lord Broadhurst. "Another cup," she said.

Janie walked with Harry down the hall. So close, she could feel the pressure of his arm against the fabric of her sleeve. She felt her fingers drifting toward his like iron filings toward a magnet.

"The entire servants' hall is buzzing," he whispered, taking her hand in his. "Everyone's talking, and I can't believe all of it is true." He studied her closely. "Are you all right?"

"I think so." She turned to face him. Looking up into his face, into the warmth of his eyes, a little tightness left her chest. "But I'm scared."

"You, Janie? Of what?" He opened the door and allowed her to step through ahead of him. Janie paused on the landing and looked down the steep flight of stairs.

"Of what happens next."

"What happens next is what happens every day. We walk downstairs. We make another cup of tea."

"But I don't —" Janie's voice caught on the shard of truth lodged in her throat. "I was wrong about this place."

Harry turned her around and pulled her up against his chest. Janie raised her head to look down the hall. To see who might be watching. But he moved so his face was right in front of hers. So all she could see were those champagne eyes.

"What do you mean?"

"Charlotte's my sister," Janie blurted and closed her eyes. "My father was the coachman. I thought he was fired because of me, but it was because of her." She leaned forward to put her forehead on his chest. "I don't belong here."

"You belong where your heart is," he said.

"That's what my mother says." Her eyes flew open and she looked up at him. "I have to see my mother."

"I think she's downstairs." Harry swallowed. "Like I said, we're all still up."

Janie turned and together they moved down the two flights to the basement. Harry knew when she needed silence. He knew she had to sort out her own thoughts before she could voice them.

And when the cacophony of the servants' hall reached them on the first-floor landing, he knew she needed to hold his hand.

"They're talking about me," she said, hesitating.

"Since when has that bothered you?" Harry asked, his lips close to her ear.

"Since forever." Janie was achingly aware of the nearness of him.

"But you always just dismissed it. Sarah and her jealousy. Tess's snide comments. Mollie leaving the worst of the pots for you to clean." He paused. "Me wanting to hold you back."

"That hurt the most," Janie admitted. "But at least I know why now."

"Oh?" Harry arched an eyebrow. "And why do you think?"

"Because you love me and wanted me all to yourself."

She reached up to kiss him once, and then leaned against him, drinking in the comforting scents of smoke and resin.

"Worse than that," she said quietly. "They're talking about Charlotte. And it won't be long before they do the math and realize I have a philandering father. And find ways for it to bring shame on my mother."

"She can take care of herself." Harry rested his chin on the top of her head. "I think Lady Charlotte can, too."

Janie knew this was true. But for one blinding instant, she wished someone would take care of her.

Then she straightened her shoulders and tucked a stray hair into her plait with her free hand. Lastly, she let go of Harry.

"I guess now is as good a time as any to face it," she said, more bravely than she felt.

"I'm right behind you," Harry murmured.

The servants' hall silenced when she walked in. Plates were scattered all over the table, nothing but crumbs left on them. Mollie had her saucer to her lips, blowing on the tea she'd poured there. Tess stood in the kitchen doorway, frowning. Resenting the fact she'd had to serve the staff's late-night tea, no doubt.

Mrs. Seward wasn't there. Of course she wasn't. She would be in the kitchen.

*Now is as good a time as any.*

Sarah sat near the head of the table on the maids' side, her mouth twisted into a half grin, half grimace. "What are you doing here?" she asked Janie. "Shouldn't you be out on the streets?"

Sarah and Tess erupted into laughter, but Mollie just stared miserably at her saucer, the tea rippling beneath her breath.

Janie cringed inwardly at the suggestion that she'd never again have a respectable job. But she didn't respond. She'd known it was coming. It was best just to let it roll over her like the tide.

"You always thought you were better than us," Sarah continued. "With your cooking and your training to be a lady's maid. And now you know the truth. She's not even a lady."

"Say what you like about me, Sarah," Janie said. "But I will not let you talk that way about my *sister.*"

Half of the faces in the room registered shock, and the other half satisfaction. Apparently, the arithmetic had already been done.

Sarah was obviously one who had already guessed. And obviously delighted in getting a rise out of Janie. "I don't see why. Neither one of you are any better than her tart of a mother. You're not even good enough for the piffling Peasgood."

The room went silent. Waiting for Janie to respond. To fly at Sarah over the table. Scratch her eyes out. Scream curses. Girls had done it before at The Manor. Living in such close quarters bred hostility.

Janie refused to give them the satisfaction.

"There you're right, Sarah," she said, letting her voice grow low and dangerous, but sweetening it as best she could. "Harry's too good for me."

She felt Harry move behind her, ready to jump in. Contradict her. But she held up a hand to stop him.

"He makes me feel like I'm better than this." She swept a hand out, encompassing the entire servants' hall. "Better than you, Sarah."

Someone hissed and Mollie dropped her saucer, but Janie didn't let them interject.

"He makes me want to be a better *person*," she said. "Someone who cares and helps and believes in what's right. It wouldn't matter if I were the scullery maid or the Duchess of Devonshire. Until I can be better than petty quarrels and the pecking order of hierarchy, I won't be worthy of him."

She looked over her shoulder and smiled. It didn't matter anymore who knew. She didn't have to keep this a secret. So she kissed him gently on the cheek and turned back to her dumbfounded audience.

"But I'm determined to keep trying."

# Chapter 21

Charlotte stood in the open door of her bedroom, waiting for Andrew Broadhurst to say something. Anything.

She imagined him telling her that none of it mattered, then stealing her away into the back of a well-appointed car and taking her to Paris, where they could elope and live happily ever after on the Left Bank.

She imagined him taking her in his arms and kissing her.

But he didn't do any of those things.

So she imagined he was wracking his brain for a good excuse to walk away. To leave her there in her room with her cup of tea. Going back to his own life, without the complications of gossip.

She imagined she had no choice but to sit and wait for her fate to be decided by others.

And then a thought struck her. Like lightning. So quick and vibrant that she jerked her head up and looked at Andrew with wild, elated eyes. His own eyes widened in surprise.

"Are you all right?" he asked.

"I'm more than all right," she said fervently. "I'm here."

Andrew looked confused, but added an encouraging smile. "I'm afraid I don't quite follow."

"Janie was right. This isn't some Gothic novel. It's real life. I'm always living inside my own head, imagining how things could be, how they *might* turn out."

Charlotte blinked and shook her head at her own folly. "I was standing here, imagining what you must be thinking. That you're trying to think of a polite way to extricate yourself from this predicament."

"I wasn't —"

"That's exactly it!" Charlotte cried, taking his hands in hers. "I don't know what you're thinking. I don't know what happens next. The only thing I have any control over is what *I* do next. I can't sit around and let someone else decide for me. All these adults who haven't even been able to figure out their own lives, much less mine. I can't live adventure inside my head. I have to go out and find it for myself."

Andrew stayed silent, his hands warm in hers. She was

completely unsure of what he would say next. She couldn't even imagine it. And she liked that.

"I don't want you to think —" She choked and stopped.

Words bottled up in Charlotte's throat, and she couldn't form them on her tongue. She didn't know how she felt about Lawrence. About how he had let her go. How he called her by someone else's name.

Andrew waited, looking at her expectantly. Not the sort of person who only listened because he was waiting to get a chance to speak. The sort of person who wanted to hear what she had to say.

Charlotte realized that how she felt — or didn't — about Lawrence didn't matter. Because what she felt about Andrew felt *true.*

"I like you," she blurted, surprising herself by saying — *and believing* — it.

Andrew smiled. "You don't want me to think you like me?"

"No!" Charlotte cried, terror seizing her, but then Andrew laughed and she found she could, too.

"I *like* you," she said again. "No matter what society says I should or shouldn't do."

"That's good," Andrew replied almost casually.

She looked up at him. At the wicked golden gleam in his dependable brown eyes. He was laughing at her.

No, he was laughing *with* her.

Andrew's gaze traveled to her lips, and Charlotte realized with a shiver that he was going to kiss her. And as the shiver descended to her feet, she realized how much she wanted him to.

His lips had almost reached hers when he murmured, "That's very good."

A movement at the end of the hall caught Charlotte's eye and propriety drew her away from him.

"You certainly work fast." Fran Caldwell still wore her beaded evening gown, but she no longer strode purposefully and her hands hung limply at her sides.

Lawrence trailed behind her, his gaze never wavering from the thick hall carpet.

Charlotte felt a flash of guilt. Her lips burned from the memory of kissing him, and her cheeks burned because Andrew had seen it.

Andrew stepped back, suddenly cool and diffident. "Miss Caldwell."

"How many more men are you going to kiss tonight, Charlotte?" Fran asked, ignoring him. "It's a good thing you've got me here to catch you. And your errant boyfriends."

Fran turned and seized Lawrence by the elbow. He didn't look up.

“See?” Fran said gleefully. “It wasn’t that hard to find him. He was already packing his bags.”

Lawrence finally met Charlotte’s eye. “I knew I’d be sacked.”

“And here I thought you’d planned to whisk her away,” Fran said. “Isn’t that what you imagined, Charlotte? In your stories? Heading off to the Côte d’Azur?”

“I didn’t —” Lawrence looked panicked, his gaze darting from Fran to Charlotte to Andrew. “I’d never —” He seemed to have trouble drawing breath.

His eyes finally came to rest on Charlotte and didn’t waver. “It was just a bit of fun.”

Out of the corner of her eye, Charlotte saw Andrew tense. And she felt her own anger squeezing inside her.

Lawrence had kissed her. Twice.

He had put her reputation and her status and her relationships with her family at risk.

The fist inside her clenched and flexed and expanded.

And escaped in a giggle. Lawrence blinked. Fran stared.

“Just a bit of fun,” Charlotte repeated, nodding. Andrew’s hands relaxed.

So Charlotte screwed hers up into a ball and punched Lawrence right in his bright blue eye. He didn’t even have time to blink.

Lawrence stumbled back, his hands up to his face.

"What the bloody letter!" he yelped, his words muffled.

"Just a bit of *fun*?" Charlotte asked. She held her hand tight against her stomach. It hurt like the dickens, but she wasn't about to let anyone know. She took a step forward.

"Like it was with Sarah?"

Lawrence's hands lowered enough for her to see the shock in his eyes.

"Like it was with *Janie*?" Charlotte stood directly in front of Lawrence and his hands fell to his sides in a helpless shrug.

Charlotte felt a surge of guilt. He had let her think she loved him.

But she hadn't.

"I deserved that," Lawrence said.

Charlotte couldn't agree with him. But the apology stuck in her throat.

"I didn't love you," she blurted.

The corner of Lawrence's mouth raised a little. "I know," he said, and cast a flickering glance at Andrew. "You deserve better."

He stepped back and straightened his waistcoat. He arranged his features into a bland footman's mask. The effect was marred by the bruise starting to bloom on his cheekbone. "Will that be all, Lady Charlotte?"

Charlotte looked at him sadly. "Yes," she said. And added, "Thank you, Lawrence."

He turned and walked away, the nipped-in waist of his tailcoat no longer enticing.

"Remind me never to get on your bad side," Andrew murmured.

And Charlotte burst into tears.

# Chapter 22

For the first time in her life, Janie didn't want to enter the kitchen. She could hear her mother rattling saucepans, clanking cutlery, and turning the taps on and off. It was late — long past the time Mrs. Seward usually went to bed — and yet she was up. Baking.

Janie closed her eyes. She breathed in the scents of cinnamon and vanilla. Cardamom and raisins.

"Are you all right?" Harry asked, resting one hand on her shoulder.

"When I go in there, everything will be different. She'll tell me what happened. And what part she played in it. Maybe she'll tell me what he was like. Or make excuses for him. Or that she didn't love him."

Janie gulped a deep breath. "Or that he didn't love me."

Harry squeezed her shoulder and whispered in her ear. "When you go in there, everything will be the same. Your mother will be baking scones." He lifted his head and sniffed once, like a pointer, and then put his lips next to her ear again. "No. Sultana cake."

Janie smiled. Sultana cake was her favorite. Somehow, her mother had gotten one to her on her birthday every year. No matter what.

Harry angled his whisper to kiss the corner of her mouth.

"Everything will be the same because she still loves you."

He squeezed her shoulder, and she stepped through the door. Mrs. Seward looked up. Her cap was slightly askew. She had flour on the end of her nose, and her eyes were rimmed with red. But she was still the same.

"Ma?"

Mrs. Seward looked up and a smile hovered at the corners of her mouth.

"Just the person I wanted to see." Her voice sounded thin.

"Why didn't you tell me?"

Mrs. Seward laid her palms flat on the table and leaned into them, hanging her head between her arms. Her shoulders rose and fell, and when she looked up again, the creases around her mouth and the circles under her eyes seemed more visible.

"They made me promise," she said. "If I wanted to come back to work here, I had to promise never to say a word."

"Why did you come back?" Janie asked. "Why would you ever come back here?"

"Because I could bring you with me."

Janie took a deep breath. Drawing in the comforting scents of baking. Of the kitchen. Of home.

"I knew you would be leaving school, Janie," Mrs. Seward went on. "And I knew things weren't easy at the farm. I couldn't let you stay there. And it was next to impossible to find a job for a cook *and* a kitchen maid."

"But I started as a scullery maid."

Mrs. Seward nodded. "This was what opened up." She reached out a hand to tuck a strand of hair back into Janie's braid. "I figured it was worth it."

Janie wrapped her arms around her mother and laid her head on Mrs. Seward's shoulder.

"And what about him?" she asked, quietly enough that her mother could pretend she didn't hear.

"I think he loved her."

Janie wanted to cry. No wonder her mother wanted to leave The Manor. *Too many memories,* she'd said.

"He died because he left here," Janie said, trying to conjure up some justifiable anger. "I don't have a father because of what she did."

"Because of what they both did."

Janie's father had always been just a story. The tale of a coachman who went into the Army to save his family.

Or to forget his past.

It seemed so long ago. It was part of Janie's life that had shaped her. The story a sequence of events that took her through poverty and drudgery and finally into the kitchen. To this very moment.

The past had shaped her, but she wanted the present to define her.

"So what happens next?" she asked.

"Why, Janie Mae," Mrs. Seward said, releasing her and brushing her hands on her apron, "we do what we do best." She swept a regal hand over the table. "We bake cakes."

"But I don't work here anymore." Janie still struggled to get the words out.

"I won't tell," Mrs. Seward said, kissing her forehead. "It will be our little secret."

"Janie," Harry said, sounding unsure.

Janie looked up at him and he nodded to the doorway, where Lord Broadhurst stood, nervously tugging on the lobe of one ear.

"How is she?" Janie asked.

"Janie Mae, you forget yourself," Mrs. Seward said, straightening her cap. "Lord Broadhurst, can we help you?"

"It's all right, Mrs. Seward. After what Janie and I have been through tonight, I think we have earned the right to dispense with formalities." Andrew turned to Janie. "Charlotte is still a trifle upset, I'm afraid. I wondered if I could trouble you for more tea." He looked at the pans and flour spread across the table. "And perhaps some more cake."

"Ma — Mrs. Seward just put a sultana cake in the oven," Janie said, taking the kettle to the cold water tap. "She makes the best in three counties."

"Her cakes are certainly the best I've ever tasted," Andrew agreed. "It's why I hope she'll be able to come to London."

Janie turned slowly. "My mother? In London?"

"I'm opening a restaurant. One that specializes in afternoon teas. I want to call it the Manor House. Let Londoners experience life in the country, right in the middle of the West End."

"She's going to work for *you*?" Janie asked. *Not Lady Beatrice.*

"I've always wanted to run my own business," Andrew said. "Combine my passions. I was going to ask Charlotte's father tomorrow." He glanced at the clock high on the kitchen wall and coughed. "Well, today. I'd hoped he'd help with an investment. And apparently Lady Diane has been planning on hiring a French chef to cook here."

"That's what you were going to ask him?" Janie asked. Not for Charlotte's hand in marriage. She wondered if Charlotte would be disappointed now. She put the kettle back down on the stove and turned to her mother. "Why didn't you tell me?"

"Because Lord Broadhurst didn't have the investment yet. I didn't want to say until it was a sure thing."

Andrew turned a little pink. "I do apologize. I seem to have let the cat out of the bag."

"Well, you're not the first person to do that tonight," Mrs. Seward said.

Her mother sounded so nonchalant. So unconcerned. As if moving to London to start a new job — a new career — didn't matter. As if Janie didn't matter. Janie didn't have a home. She didn't have a job. She had nothing.

Janie had assumed that her mother *couldn't* take her along if she worked for Lady Beatrice. But a restaurant kitchen needed more than one person.

"When were you going to tell me?" Janie blurted. "When you left? Or when I came begging you for a job because I was starving on the streets?"

Everyone fell silent.

"Or were you just going to keep it a secret forever, like the fact that I have a sister?" Janie couldn't stop once she started. It was like a tap had been turned and everything came spewing forth. "What I don't know can't hurt me, right? Did you think I wouldn't notice when my *mother* disappeared and I was suddenly working for a Frenchman? Or when I lost my job and had nowhere to go?"

Her voice lost all its strength as a sob rose in her throat and stifled her.

Harry's hand found its way into hers.

Andrew opened his mouth as if to respond, but Mrs. Seward held up a finger to silence him.

"There was another offer," she said.

"So I get your castoffs?" Janie asked, unwilling to let the argument go.

"It was an offer for you," Mrs. Seward said. "And only for you."

Janie let that information settle low in her heart. And waited.

"But I knew how much you love it here, so I wasn't going to mention it to you." Mrs. Seward sighed. "And because it will take you far away. So far, I won't get to see you. At least if you worked in a country house you might come into town for the Season."

"How far?" Janie asked warily.

"Italy." Mrs. Seward sighed again and didn't look up from the leaves at the bottom of her teacup, as if she were trying to read her fortune in them. Her face looked tired. "Lady Beatrice wants you to be her cook."

# Chapter 23

Charlotte's eyes felt swollen shut, and her throat burned. When she turned her head, there was a wet spot on her pillow. And her hand hurt.

Then she remembered. Lawrence. The lake. Her mother. Mother*s*, plural.

But she also remembered Andrew. His picking her up for the third time that night and carrying her to her bed. Feeding her tea and fruitcake. And sitting in the overstuffed chair by her bed. Watching until she fell asleep.

Charlotte pried one eye open a crack. The chair was empty. And the light parting the curtains was stabbingly bright.

She wondered what would happen if she just pretended not to wake up.

But she was through with imagining her life.

She needed to see her mother. Both of them. She needed to thank Andrew.

*And she needed to talk to Janie before she left.* Lady Diane didn't tolerate dismissed servants remaining at The Manor, not even if they had no place to go.

Charlotte swung her legs out of the bed, her head swimming. She still wore her tea gown from the night before. Without thinking, Charlotte reached for the bell pull and stopped when her hand gripped the velvet.

Sarah had refused to come upstairs the night before. Why should today be any different?

"Blast." Tears threatened again. She couldn't even dress herself. Couldn't tighten the corset. Could barely do her hair. She was tired of being helpless. Tired of being useless.

"I'll just have to go in this."

Charlotte searched for stockings and slippers. She ran the brush through her hair, remembering Janie doing it. How she felt even then that it was something a sister would do. Quickly, she twisted her hair into a knot and stabbed it with pins. It would have to suffice.

She strode across the room and threw open the door, only to find Fran on the other side, her hand raised to knock.

Charlotte sagged. "Why are you here?"

"All the other guests have left." Fran wouldn't look Charlotte in the eye.

Charlotte felt even more deflated. That meant the gossip had already started. And Andrew was gone, as well.

"So did you come here to gloat?" Charlotte asked. "It's too early for a fight."

But Fran didn't have the air of someone looking for a fight. She looked like someone with all the fight knocked out of her.

"I came to apologize," she said.

"For what?" Though a dozen answers came to Charlotte immediately.

"For everything. I — I wanted you to get caught," Fran said. "You were throwing your life away."

"It's my life," Charlotte said, and realized she liked the sound of that.

"I just didn't want you to tarnish your chances, Charlotte. I was a good friend."

Charlotte snorted in disbelief. "I'd hate to see how you treat your enemies."

"There's more to love than hugs and kisses, you know. There's protecting somebody. Even if it means protecting her from herself."

Charlotte wondered if that's what Lady Diane had thought she was doing. For Charlotte. For Beatrice.

"I wanted what was best for you," Fran continued, as ever without waiting for a response.

But Charlotte was tired of people not wanting to hear what she had to say. She took a step closer to Fran and raised her voice. "What *you* thought was best. What my mother thought was best."

"Because in our society that *is* what's best!"

"The world is changing, Fran. And we're going to have to change with it. Act as individuals instead of part of the herd. Especially if the herd excludes most of the people in the country."

"Are you saying I should consort with the staff?" Fran sniped. "Learn how to make my own toast? Have a job? I think not."

"And that's why we're different, Fran. I want to know how to do things. I want to be able to dress and feed myself. I want to have my own ideas. And I *want* to have a job. I want to be a writer."

"Good luck finding a man who will tolerate that."

Charlotte froze for a moment, thinking of Andrew. Of his determination that everyone should have the vote. Of his interest in her stories. Of the shared humor in his dark eyes.

But he'd left. The thought caused more pain than she would have imagined possible a few days before.

Charlotte took a deep breath. "Then I'll just have to keep looking until I find one."

Fran pinched her upper lip between her teeth. She didn't look like she would toss her head and make a judgment without batting an eye. She looked on the verge of tears herself.

"I guess I just don't believe that's possible," she said. "All I ever wanted was what you have. The title. The Manor. The parties. The Season."

"Is that the only reason you were after David?" Charlotte asked.

Fran shrugged like it was nothing. "At least I'd know what to expect."

"But now you can expect nothing," Charlotte said harshly. "Because The Manor is in disrepute."

Fran hung her head. "I thought if I caught you with the footman, you'd see how stupid you were being. I wasn't going to tell anyone. Really."

"You brought Andrew with you."

"I knew Lord Broadhurst would be too much of a gentleman to stoop to tittle-tattle."

"You told my *mother*."

"Because you ran away!" Fran cried, looking up. Her eyes

were rimmed with red. "I didn't know what else to do. You ran off into the dark. It was terrifying."

It was liberating.

"At least it taught me who my friends really are," Charlotte said. "And if you don't mind, I need to catch her before she leaves."

Charlotte brushed past Fran and strode down the hall to the servants' stairs.

"The kitchen maid?" Fran was right on her heels.

"Janie." Charlotte used her fingertips to pry open the hidden door.

The stairwell was dark and smelled of wood and sweat. And the odors escaping the kitchen — bacon and deviled kidneys and freshly baked scones.

"Is it true she's your half sister?"

Charlotte stopped and turned back. Janie was right. Gossip traveled quickly in The Manor.

"Sister," she corrected.

"No wonder you liked her so much better than me."

Charlotte was suddenly tired of Fran's self-absorption and emotional manipulations.

"I liked Janie because she didn't pretend to be anything other than what she was," Charlotte said. "And because knowing her gave me courage to be who *I* am."

"I thought she was a bad influence on you." Fran paused and looked at Charlotte sadly. "But I guess I was wrong."

"Yes, you were." Charlotte turned back to where the stairs descended into pitch darkness. On the wall was a narrow shelf, holding a candle and a box of matches. Unlike Charlotte, The Manor servants prepared for every eventuality.

Fran didn't move while Charlotte struck the match, but then said, "I'd like to meet her."

Charlotte scrutinized her over the flame.

"Fine," she said and led the way down the stairs.

There were voices coming from the servants' hall when they got down to the basement. Charlotte could hear Sarah distinctly.

"Well, I for one am not serving the illegitimate daughter of a coachman."

The words stopped Charlotte dead, one foot on the brick floor of the hall, the other toe still resting on the bottom stair. As the truth hit her, she found she no longer had the courage to move forward.

Fran put a hand on her back. "This isn't the worst you're going to hear. But you're strong enough not to let it get to you."

As angry as she still was at Fran, those words comforted her.

"I don't know why Lord Broadhurst is sticking around," a male voice said.

Charlotte gasped and looked back over her shoulder. "Andrew's still here?"

Fran nodded. "I guess you know who your friends are."

Charlotte felt a flare of joy until another voice rang out of the servants' hall. "I always knew there was summat wrong with her."

Fran pushed down the stairs and marched up to the door to the hall. There was a scraping of chairs and clanging of crockery as the servants all stood.

"I'm looking for a cup of tea," Fran announced.

Again, chairs scraped and clatter ensued and several voices said at once, "I can get that for you, Miss Caldwell."

"No," Fran said sharply. "I'm afraid you misunderstand me. I'm looking for someone to help me and my friend — Lady Charlotte — get a cup of tea and maybe a piece of cake. Can anyone tell me where Janie Seward is?"

Silence.

A shadow flickered on the doorjamb on the other side of Fran and Charlotte thought she saw a face looking out at her, wide-eyed.

Then a simple statement from deep within the servants' hall. "She's in the kitchen. Just saying good-bye to her mother."

# Chapter 24

Janie stoked the giant coal-burning stove, knowing it would probably be the last time. Harry stood behind her, leaning back on the great oak table. Like nothing had changed.

"You're beautiful," he said. "You know that?"

*That* was different. And Janie found that she liked it.

"As only a girl with her head in an oven can be," she called into the burner. The heat flared, and she moved back, feeling the surge on the thin skin of her cheeks.

"You are," Harry said as she stood up, dusting her hands together. He grabbed them before she wiped them on her apron.

Only she wasn't wearing an apron. She was wearing her traveling dress.

"Oh!" Janie cried and looked up at him. "Thanks for that."

He pressed her palms against his chest to get the coal dust off of them and pulled her closer.

"I mean it," he murmured into her ear, causing a little shiver to trail down her spine. "I don't care if you're in a Worth gown or covered in grease and cream, you're beautiful."

And Janie smiled up at him — because she believed him.

"No more of that now, chickens, we don't want you getting sacked twice from the same job." Mrs. Seward stepped in through the courtyard door.

Janie dropped her hands.

"I was just making tea," Janie said.

"You were just doing more than that, Janie Mae."

"I didn't think . . ."

"You're still under Lady Diane's roof and though she's still . . . indisposed, she has a very long arm and very little tolerance."

Janie nodded, peeping at Harry out of the corner of her eye. He looked terrified. But when she turned back to her mother, Mrs. Seward's shoulders were shaking, her lips pressed tightly together.

"You're laughing?" Janie cried.

"It's about time the two of you stopped pretending there was nothing between you." Mrs. Seward picked up the empty kettle from the kitchen table and held it out to Janie pointedly, still chuckling.

They hadn't talked about what would happen next. Janie wasn't sure she wanted to work for Lady Beatrice. Or move to Italy. It would take several months to establish the Manor House restaurant in London, and her mother wouldn't need kitchen staff until it opened. Janie knew she couldn't remain at The Manor. She'd probably already overstayed her welcome, having spent the night. She could get a train to New Romney, and from there walk the two and a half miles to her uncle's farm. They wouldn't turn her away, but with no job and no character reference, she'd just be a burden.

Janie traced a finger along the grain of the scarred oak table.

"I'm going to miss it," she said.

Mrs. Seward laid her hand over Janie's, stilling it.

"There is an entire world out there, my girl. This is not all there is."

Janie thought of the view of the hills from the kitchen gate. She thought of the mud between her toes down at the lake. She thought of early mornings, alone with Harry, the two of them working together before anyone else awoke.

She couldn't imagine the entire world.

She heard the scraping and clatter from the servants' hall. And she heard what Miss Caldwell said next. She pressed her lips together as she watched Miss Caldwell lead Charlotte into the kitchen.

"I hear you're looking for tea," Janie said.

Harry stepped up next to her, his arm pressing hers lightly.

"I hear you're Charlotte's sister." Miss Caldwell tossed her head.

Janie nodded.

Miss Caldwell took a deep breath, and a glimmer of doubt crossed her expression. Then she stuck out her hand.

"I'm Frances Caldwell," she said. "Charlotte's . . . friend." She cast a questioning look in Charlotte's direction. "I hope."

Janie stared at the hand. And then shook it.

"Janie Seward." She smiled wryly. "Former kitchen maid."

"I know who you are," Fran said. She looked Janie up and down. "And you're more than a kitchen maid. You're an adventuress. At least in Charlotte's stories."

Janie looked at Charlotte. "You wrote about me?"

"I was always the helpless maiden, getting rescued," Charlotte said. "You were the girl warrior. Doing all the things I couldn't imagine myself doing. Fighting your own battles. Rescuing yourself."

Janie wanted to be the sort of person Charlotte thought she was.

"They were all you, Charlotte," Fran said, swiping a hot scone off the tray. "You just didn't realize it."

As Janie watched her, grinning around a mouthful of scone, a series of images flashed through her mind. Fran sneaking looks at Charlotte's desk. Charlotte throwing the pages in the wastebasket. Janie taking them downstairs and hiding them. A flash of pink at the kitchen window.

"How do you know?" Janie asked.

Fran stopped chewing and appeared to have difficulty swallowing.

"Know what?" she asked.

"What Charlotte wrote."

"You read it." Charlotte stepped forward to look Fran in the eye. "I didn't realize it last night. I was so . . . confused. But you knew about Lawrence, too. The Italian count. The Côte d'Azur."

Fran shrugged minutely.

"I gave it to Janie for safekeeping," Charlotte persisted, a deep V creasing between her eyebrows and her arms stiff at her sides.

"And you found it in the cookery book," Janie finished.

Fran looked at Charlotte's hands — tightening against her skirts — and took a step back. "I was curious."

"You showed them to Mrs. Griffiths," Janie said, nearly breathless with anger. "You said they were mine. You almost got me sacked."

"Mrs. Griffiths caught me in here," Fran said, her voice a thready imitation of its usual penetrating timbre. "All I said was that you hid them."

"I blamed *Harry*!" Janie cried.

"Mother almost burned them." Charlotte's voice was flat with anger.

Fran pressed up against the table behind her. "I didn't know that. I didn't know any of it. I wasn't supposed to be snooping, was I?"

"So you couldn't just tell the truth?" Janie asked.

"No one else does in this house," Fran snapped. "I don't see why I should."

"Maybe it's time we started," said a new voice from the doorway. Lady Beatrice.

Charlotte turned so quickly she almost fell. Fran caught her elbow, and Janie steadied Charlotte on the other side. The two girls looked at each other. Janie wanted to finish the argument, but realized there were more important matters at hand.

Charlotte needed all the support she could get. Even if it came from Frances Caldwell.

"Forgive me for interrupting," Lady Beatrice said. Her chin tilted up slightly, as if she were feigning confidence. "But I came in search of my daughter."

# Chapter 25

When Charlotte had been a child, she'd imagined she was someone else's daughter. Like Rapunzel or the Stolen Child by Yeats. As she whiled away long hours in the nursery — never allowed to come out because her mother didn't want a little barefoot dervish downstairs — she told herself stories. Of the day her real mother came to get her.

None of the stories were anything like this.

"Why are you here?" she asked Beatrice. She couldn't think of her as *Mother.* She didn't feel any connection to this woman.

Beatrice's chin dropped, like the air had been knocked out of her. Mrs. Seward turned away, clattering spoons and banging the kettle.

"I wanted to see you," Beatrice said, and flicked a glance

at Mrs. Seward's back. "And I wanted to make amends. It was my fault."

"Yes, it was your fault," Charlotte heard herself say, her tone not half as angry as she wanted it to be. "It was your fault Mrs. Seward had to leave her place here. It was your fault Janie grew up without her mother. It's your fault my mother is the way she is — so full of rules and what people think that she can't see the real people living under her own roof."

"I'm afraid Diane was a bit like that before," Beatrice said. "She has an active imagination, and wants to do everything she can to prevent all those fictitious scenarios from happening."

Charlotte stared, her thoughts ticking over like a clock with faulty gears. They kept sliding backward into the same place.

Lady Diane imagined what could happen and spent all her energy making sure it didn't.

Charlotte imagined what could happen and spent all her energy wishing that it would.

Neither one lived in the present. Neither one dealt with life as it truly was.

Beatrice stepped into the room, but not far enough to be part of the circle. Fran and Janie still flanked Charlotte, and Harry stood on Janie's other side, his left hand covering her right on the edge of the oak table.

"I think Diane wanted to be a writer, too," Beatrice said softly. "But she eventually saw all the shameful possibilities and talked herself out of it."

"And what about you?" Charlotte asked.

"All I ever wanted was adventure."

There it was. The connection.

"And you found it," Charlotte said.

"But I went too far." Beatrice stepped closer to the table. "Diane always worried too much about rules and appearances, so I was determined not to care. To do what I wanted, despite what other people thought." She looked sadly at Mrs. Seward, who stood to one side, watching. "Or suffered."

Mrs. Seward smiled tightly.

Charlotte felt spite coiling in her chest.

"So you came back to what?" she asked. "To make amends? To apologize so we'll all be a happy family? I don't know if that's possible. You saddled my mother with an unwanted baby, and now you've ruined her social status as well. It's all she ever cared about." Charlotte had to take a breath, and then another because the first one caught in her throat. "And what about me? Did you just expect me to welcome you with open arms?"

"No!" Beatrice said loudly, startling them all. "I expected nothing of the sort!" She looked about at all their faces. "I don't expect any of you to forgive me." She stopped in front of Charlotte and looked at her steadily. "Though I hope you will. Eventually."

Silence descended on the little group, and Charlotte imagined herself saying the words that would bring them all to a happy ending. But she couldn't.

So instead she said, "I'll try."

And Beatrice nodded her understanding, her eyes glassy with unshed tears.

"I'd like you to come with me," she said. "To Italy."

Charlotte didn't respond. She just stared at the great oak table.

Janie squeezed her arm. "It would be an adventure."

The air around Charlotte stilled, and suddenly she was overly sensitive to everything in the room. To the cut of the teacup's rim beneath her finger. The shallow *drip* that came from the scullery. The heat of the oven on the other side of the room.

"An adventure," she repeated.

She could leave The Manor. Get out of her mother's sphere of influence. Make some of her own choices. Experience another country — another culture.

Write.

Terror fluttered in her throat. Adventure was for the imagination.

Wasn't it?

"But —" she stuttered and looked up at the woman in front of her. "I don't know you."

Lady Beatrice cocked her head to one side. "You could get to know me."

Charlotte paused. She thought about Andrew. How she'd always assumed he was boring. But he wasn't. She looked at Janie, and remembered what she'd said the night she taught Charlotte the hesitation waltz.

*Sometimes people aren't what you think they are at first.*

Maybe Beatrice wasn't an adventuress. But maybe she wasn't just a selfish deserter, either. Maybe she was somewhere in between. Charlotte would never know if she didn't try.

She studied Beatrice. Her blonde hair. Her hazel eyes.

"What did he look like?" she asked.

Beatrice bit her lip and glanced quickly at Mrs. Seward. She regarded Janie for a moment, and then turned back to Charlotte.

"He looked like both of you," she said, finally. "He had red hair and greenish eyes. And a nose that just started to turn up at the end."

Sarah clattered into the doorway and stopped short, frowning at the collection of people in the kitchen.

"Lady Diane is awake," she said, and her gaze finally landed on Charlotte. "She wants to see you."

A trickle of fear slid down Charlotte's throat. She had no idea what to expect from Lady Diane. Or even what she expected in return.

She was essentially free from all the rules and obligations heaped upon a daughter of The Manor. She no longer *had* to do what Lady Diane said. But the woman who raised her deserved her respect at the very least.

"Now," Sarah said. It looked like she was restraining herself from stamping her foot.

Charlotte refocused on the housemaid. The girl who had helped her dress and done her hair for years. And who now treated her like she was undesirable. Charlotte could see what Andrew meant about the injustice of class distinctions. That people should be judged on their integrity and not their social standing.

"One moment, Sarah," Charlotte said, and turned to Janie. "You'll still be here?"

"I have a train to catch."

"But you can't," Charlotte said. "You can't just leave."

"I'm still hoping to persuade Janie to come and work for me," Beatrice said.

Janie? Charlotte looked at her friend — her *sister.* They could be together. Just like she'd imagined.

"I haven't decided," Janie said, her words rushed, and turned to Beatrice. "I don't know when you're leaving." She paused. "And I can't stay here."

Sarah — still in the doorway — made a *humph*ing sound. But when Beatrice glared at her, the housemaid widened her eyes in mock innocence.

"Lord Edmonds has agreed to let me make some of the household decisions while my sister is . . . indisposed," Beatrice said, turning back to Janie and Charlotte. "I think you should stay here for at least another day, Janie. With your mother."

Charlotte moved to the door, keeping her eyes on Janie. "Please." She looked at Sarah's already disappearing form, and then back again. "For me."

After Janie nodded, Charlotte followed Sarah down the basement passageway and out through the door that opened beneath the grand staircase in the marble hall. Charlotte tried not to listen to the echoing of their footsteps. Tried not to remember Lady Diane's voice ringing across it. Or the shocked stares of all the guests.

At the top of the stairs, Sarah turned left, away from Charlotte's room. They passed paintings by Turner, Gainsborough, and Brueghel. Charlotte hadn't been down this hall since she was a child and her nanny would walk her past all these terrifying faces and landscapes after tea.

Back then, Lady Diane would be waiting to inspect Charlotte's clothes, her hair, her fingernails. She'd ask for a recitation of a poem or, later, how to address a marquess in person or a viscount in writing. And then Charlotte would be dismissed. All parental interaction done for the day.

Sarah knocked at the broad white door and opened it when a voice inside called, "Enter." But she let Charlotte go in alone and closed the door behind her.

Lady Diane lay on a chaise by the window, looking out across the lawn and graveled drive. Toward the lake. She looked . . . smaller. Her hair was down around her shoulders, brushed, but coarse with gray. Her eyes had deep bruise-like circles under them.

Charlotte didn't know what to say. She wasn't even sure she was allowed to speak. The silence between them throbbed.

"What were you doing down at the lake?" Lady Diane finally asked.

Charlotte startled. Of all the questions to be asked, this was the last one she expected.

"I was going to —" Charlotte stopped. None of it mattered anymore.

"Run away?"

Charlotte nodded.

"Speak, Charlotte, you're not a mute."

"Yes."

Lady Diane waited. And then turned back to the window.

"I suppose I can't expect you to call me Mother anymore."

Charlotte swallowed. "No."

Lady Diane closed her eyes, as if the glare from the morning sun was too much for her.

Charlotte quelled a surge of guilt. "Aunt —" She paused. "Beatrice invited me to go to Italy with her."

Lady Diane didn't open her eyes. "I know."

In the past, Lady Diane would have told Charlotte what to do. What to think. How to feel. And though independence was what she wanted, Charlotte wasn't entirely comfortable having to do all of those things for herself. It was just so . . . difficult.

"I'm thinking of taking her up on it." The statement surprised her. Until she said it out loud, she hadn't been sure if she wanted to go. "It might be good for me to get to know my . . . my mother."

Lady Diane turned back to Charlotte and fixed her with those steely blue eyes. Charlotte held her breath. Waiting for judgment.

"You're wrong," Lady Diane said quietly.

Charlotte wasn't surprised to hear this about the first decision she'd been asked to make on her own. She felt the ball of anger curling in her chest again. She forced herself to return Lady Diane's gaze and say, "Then I guess I'll just have to learn from my mistakes."

Lady Diane turned swiftly on her chaise and leaned forward, her body emphasizing the strength of her conviction. "I didn't mean about going to Italy, Charlotte. That's your decision to make. And I trust you're smart enough to make the right one."

Charlotte blinked in surprise. "Then what?" she blurted. "What was I wrong about?"

"When you said I didn't love you," Lady Diane said. "You are my only daughter. And I love you as best I can."

Charlotte wondered if this was good enough, and then realized it would have to be. "Just because you love someone doesn't mean you can change her into the person you imagine she should be," she said finally.

"Maybe if I had allowed you to make a few mistakes early on, you wouldn't have . . ."

"I would still be me," Charlotte said. "Though I can't say whether or not I would have kissed a footman."

She swallowed, waiting for the dressing-down that was sure to follow that statement. But Lady Diane coughed a laugh.

"I've been told he has quite a shiner this morning."

Charlotte almost laughed herself. "Really, Mother. Slang."

Lady Diane's eyes filled with tears. Charlotte had never seen that before, and didn't know what to do or say. Didn't even know what to do with her hands.

"Thank you, Charlotte," Lady Diane said. "For calling me Mother."

# Chapter 26

Janie didn't know how to be still. How to do nothing. Without a job to do, she felt useless. So she sat in the shade of the courtyard gate, watching deliverymen come and go and the sunlight bleach the hills of the Weald.

Harry bumped her hip on the upturned barrel and she moved over so he could perch next to her.

"They've given me my job back," he said.

Janie looked at him in surprise. "How did you manage that?"

"Good hall boys are hard to find," Harry said.

"Especially those who can repair any piece of machinery in The Manor."

"They made me promise to avoid all contact with the maids." Harry grinned, the freckles on his cheek disappearing into a dimple.

"That must have been a hardship."

Harry looked at her seriously and rested one hand on her cheek. "It was the easiest promise I ever made."

Janie kissed him, unable to find the words.

"Janie Mae!" Mrs. Seward stood in the kitchen doorway, her hands on her hips. "Lady Beatrice wants to talk to you." She raised an eyebrow at the two of them, and shook her head, chuckling.

Janie stood. Looked at Harry. She didn't know if she wanted to go to Italy. So far away.

"Your hands are shaking." Harry took them between his own.

"I'm all right." Janie tried a smile. It hurt.

"I'll walk you in." Harry kept hold of her right hand and led her across the courtyard and into the basement hall. She let go of Harry's hand. She didn't need to follow the rules anymore, but Harry did.

"What do you think you'll do?" Harry asked as they passed the footman's closet. Foyle was fitting a livery jacket on the new footman — a tall blond with prominent cheekbones and a quirky smile.

"I don't know," Janie said. "Going back to Romney Marsh and then working for Ma and Lord Broadhurst seems the safest option."

She'd be with her mother.

She'd be closer to Harry.

Harry stopped at the bottom of the stairs. "Do you need me to dare you?" he asked. "Because I will, you know."

"Your dares always get me into trouble, Harry Peasgood."

"Sometimes trouble is worth the risk."

Janie swallowed the lump that threatened to rise in her throat.

"What about you?" She scurried up the short flight of stairs to the door behind the grand staircase and turned around. "Where will you go?"

"I'll stay here," he said, joining her on the narrow landing. "Someone once told me the place would fall apart without Harry Peasgood."

"But you never wanted to stay."

"I have a reason to now. You'll know where to find me." Harry brushed a strand of hair off of her temple and pressed his lips in its place. "I'll wait."

"Come with me."

Harry laughed and opened the door. "Lady Beatrice hires only women."

"No, now. Come with me now to speak to her."

"I can't." Harry spread his arms. His hands were dirty, and his cambric shirt was faded and had no collar, much less a tie. His suspenders were crooked and the knee of his trousers had worn almost all the way through, but his shoes were highly polished.

Harry caught her staring. "I don't mind the polishing. It's methodical, you know? Lets me think."

Janie nodded. She understood completely.

"I think you look wonderful, Harry," she said. "And I'd like you to come with me."

Janie led the way to the sitting room. Lady Diane still felt too unwell to come downstairs. Janie suspected that she just didn't want to face the neighbors.

Lady Beatrice stood by the French doors, looking out over the drive. Charlotte and Andrew sat on opposite ends of a small settee. Their hands were so close together they could have touched.

Or perhaps they had been.

Andrew leapt to his feet.

"Miss Seward," he said. "Always a pleasure."

"Lord Broadhurst. I'm glad you're still here."

"I was presumptuous enough to ask to stay the night," Andrew said. "So I can say good-bye."

Charlotte was studying her hands, clasped tightly in her lap.

"You're going?" Janie asked her. "To Italy?"

"She has conditions." Lady Beatrice turned from the window. She looked even younger. Lighter. As if revealing her secrets had lifted years from her face and weight from her shoulders.

"Conditions?" Janie asked.

"I told Beatrice I wouldn't go if you didn't," Charlotte said. It didn't escape Janie's notice that she didn't use the word *mother*. Not yet, anyway.

Janie stiffened. "I haven't decided."

"I know," Charlotte said, jumping off the settee and walking to her. "So Beatrice and I have been talking about it. I said it seemed unfair. We're sisters. I didn't like the idea of me being some kind of lady of the house while you slaved away."

"I like the work," Janie said.

"I told Charlotte she had the wrong idea about my house," Beatrice interjected. "I'm going to put her to work, too. I need to take best advantage of both of your talents."

Janie exchanged a look with Charlotte, who suppressed a grin.

"Talents?" Janie asked.

"Janie, you're a cook," Beatrice said, picking up a piece of Battenburg cake from the tray on the spindly table near her. "And a very good one at that." She took a bite and swallowed. "And Charlotte is a writer."

Janie stared dumbly.

"I believe in equal rights for women," Beatrice elaborated. "It's one of the reasons I run a household with only women in it. We work as hard and are at least as clever as men. And I think by alerting the world to that fact, we can make a difference."

"You're a suffragette?" Janie said, thinking of women chaining themselves to wrought iron gates and being force-fed in prison.

"I believe in women's suffrage," Beatrice said. "I believe in suffrage for all adults." She nodded at Harry. "But I also believe in opportunities. Women will get the right to vote, and soon, I hope. But it may be longer before women are treated equally. I intend to do that as best I can. And to show that it can be done."

Beatrice smiled at Charlotte. "That's where Charlotte comes in. She can help me to describe the world as it is. Or imagine it as it could be. Our house will — I hope — be completely equal. There will have to be rules, of course, but I'm hoping we will establish them together."

A flutter began in Janie's stomach and she looked at Beatrice directly. "Will my ma be able to come and visit?"

"Whenever she wishes. And we'll hopefully divide our time between Italy and my London house."

"And Harry?" Janie asked. She didn't even have to look at him to find his hand. "I can't live in another house that doesn't allow me to see him." The flutter turned into a tremble and Harry squeezed her hand.

"If there's one thing I've learned in my life," Beatrice said, "it's that there's no way to regulate falling in love."

"Or with whom," Charlotte said and looked at Andrew.

"And what about your mother?" Janie asked. "Lady Diane," she clarified. She knew this touched a tender bruise on Charlotte. But she had to ask it, or Charlotte might regret her decision.

"She says she'll come and visit when she's well," Charlotte said. "It may be good for her to get away. From the scandal."

"Is that why you're going?"

Charlotte laughed. "You certainly can be blunt, Janie." She looked at Beatrice. "But no. I'm going because I want to."

"Good," Janie said, the flutter increasing and expanding until she could barely squeeze her words around it. "Then I'm going with you."

Charlotte hugged her, bouncing up and down on her toes. Beatrice surprised her by kissing her lightly on the cheek. And Andrew shook her hand.

He held it a moment too long, then leaned closer.

"Take care of her, Janie," he whispered.

"Of course I will," Janie said, and added confidingly, "But I don't think she'll need it."

"I'm inclined to believe you're right."

Beatrice rang for tea. "You must stay, Janie. And Harry, too."

Janie looked at where Harry stood, his hands clamped to his sides so he didn't make any marks on the upholstery.

"Thank you, Lady Beatrice —" Janie began.

"Just Beatrice. You and Charlotte must both call me Beatrice."

"Thank you, Beatrice." Janie glanced again at Harry and almost laughed. He looked so much more at home in the kitchen. Probably as she herself did. "But I think I should go speak with my mother."

The servants' stairs and basement passageway were exactly the same going down as they had been going up, but they looked completely different to Janie. She noticed the scuff marks on the stairs, the scratch on the big hall bell, the single missing leather bucket from the line that hung all the way down the hall, filled with sand in case of a fire.

Janie paused in the kitchen doorway, unable to quell the pulse of homesickness that throbbed in her veins.

Mrs. Seward looked up from the chocolate cake she was glazing. Janie knew that the expression on her own face — and probably Harry's — told the whole story. But Janie needed to say it out loud. To make it real.

"I'm going to Italy."

Her mother walked around the table, wrapped Janie in a hug, and then held her at arm's length.

"You're sure?" Mrs. Seward asked. "You know I'd have you in my kitchen anytime."

Janie suddenly wanted to accept. To take the safe option. To refuse Harry's dare.

But she shook her head. "I know," she said. "But I think I'm ready for this."

Mrs. Seward hugged her again and whispered in her ear, "I *know* you are."

Pans crashed and rattled in the scullery and Janie laughed. "Do you need some help?"

"I just need to finish this cake. I'm going to send it to Miss Caldwell as a peace offering."

Janie scowled.

"None of that, my dear. We all make mistakes." Mrs. Seward looked over Janie's shoulder to where Harry stood. Waiting. "And false accusations." She took Janie's chin in her hand. "Everyone deserves a little forgiveness, don't you think?"

Janie nodded.

"Now go out and get a little fresh air." Mrs. Seward turned back to the table. "I think the weather's beginning to break."

Harry walked Janie all the way to the edge of the lawn. To where the ha-ha dropped away into the meadow beyond. They stood on the verge, facing each other. Not touching. Just looking. Janie studied him. Memorized him. The light hazel eyes, the freckles, the nose — a little short and rounded at the end — the straight jaw. And those curls.

"I'll miss you," she said.

Harry put his hand over his heart. "Part of me will be with you wherever you go."

"I love you," she said helplessly.

"I know," he replied, pulling her into an embrace. "Which is why you need to start this adventure so I can eventually become a part of it."

# Chapter 27

Charlotte tugged at the hem of her lilac-colored basque jacket and looked out at the view. The morning light brushed the tops of the hedgerows and the air felt clean and cool. Two cars waited on the gravel drive. One — a dependable Rolls-Royce Silver Ghost — would take Andrew to London, where he would begin work on his new endeavor. The Manor's green Daimler waited to make the short trip to Penshurst station, where a train would whisk her into her new life.

Charlotte turned and looked down the drive to the courtyard gate. Janie stood there with a carpetbag, Harry by her side and Mrs. Seward right behind her. Janie hugged her mother, kissed Harry quickly, and started to walk up the long drive toward the cars alone.

Lady Beatrice came out onto the porch and Charlotte started down the front entrance steps.

"We'll all use the same door, won't we?" Charlotte asked, pausing on the bottom step and looking up at Beatrice. "At your house?"

"When we come from town, we'll use the front," Beatrice said, joining her. "When we come from the garden, we'll use the back. All of us."

"Good," Charlotte said, still looking up at The Manor. The limestone and brick, the bay-fronted sitting room, the windows glinting reflections of the green summer air.

"I wish she had come down to say good-bye."

"My sister was never good at good-byes."

Beatrice looked up as well, and then nodded her chin at one of the sky-colored windows.

"She's watching," Beatrice said, and kissed Charlotte on the cheek. "Perhaps that means she'll be good at hellos when the time comes."

The tightness didn't leave Charlotte's chest, but she nodded and said, "I hope so."

They turned together and saw Andrew standing by the door of his car.

Waiting.

"I may not have a writer's eye," Beatrice whispered, "but I think that boy fancies you."

Charlotte felt the color rush up her throat and into her face, bringing with it a giddy smile. She couldn't take her eyes off Andrew as he walked toward them.

"I hope so," she murmured.

Andrew opened the rear door of the Daimler and helped Beatrice step up onto the running board. He waited until she was settled before he walked back to Charlotte, standing closer than propriety should have allowed. The tickle of his breath on her hair sent a little shiver to the nape of her neck. It was quickly followed by a chill that spread through her stomach. She looked up at him.

"I'm scared," she said.

His expression lost any trace of mirth and he studied her seriously.

"You're starting a new life," he said. "One that you will control. Making your own choices is a scary thing."

"What if I make the wrong one?"

"Then you'll learn from it. Just like your mothers did."

Charlotte's eyes burned, and she had to close them. Two mothers. Each of them loving her differently.

"I hope I don't make the same mistakes," she said.

"You'll make others."

Charlotte opened her eyes, and his were laughing at her again. Then the intensity behind them became more refined, more focused. More serious.

"I refuse to avoid making choices because I might make mistakes," Andrew said. "I want to choose where my life will go. And with whom I fall in love."

His eyes didn't leave hers as he added, "I think I may be falling in love with you."

Charlotte hoped that her eyes told him all she wanted to say. Because she found that all she *could* say was:

"Oh."

He must have heard something in that *oh* because he took one step closer and kissed her softly on the lips. A kiss so unlike Lawrence's that it felt like her first. Because this kiss wasn't just a kiss. It was a promise of more to come.

Charlotte knew she could imagine many more years of those kisses. But she chose to enjoy the moment as it happened.

"I will see you in London," Andrew said when he pulled away. Then he smiled mischievously. "And you never know. I hear the call of Florence and it is like a siren's song. I might not be able to stay away."

"I hope you don't," Charlotte said, and then laughed at herself. "Stay away, that is."

"You forget," he said. "I know how to fly an airplane. I'll be there sooner than you think."

He kissed her once more and helped her into the car. Charlotte reached for Beatrice's hand and squeezed it as Andrew shut the door.

Janie climbed into the front seat and turned around to face them. "Are you ready?"

Charlotte heard the fear in her voice. And the eagerness.

"Yes," Charlotte said. "Adventure awaits. Let's meet it together."

# Acknowledgments

Before anyone else, I would like to thank you, dear reader, for picking up this book and spending some time in the life of The Manor. Writing a book can be a lonely business, and I'm so glad you're out there at the other end of the process.

This book would never have been written without the cleverness and creativity of my editor, Aimee Friedman, or the support of my agent, Catherine Drayton. Thank you, ladies, for the journey.

I'd also like to thank the Splinters, who read my messy first draft and supplied insightful feedback and margaritas. Kristen Crowley Held, Beth Hull, and Talia Vance — I dedicate all manner of secrets to you. And a vast debt of gratitude is owed to the YA Muses (Bret Ballou, Donna Cooner,

Veronica Rossi, and Ms. Vance *again*), who kept me going through deadlines and crises of confidence.

Huge kudos to the team at Scholastic: production editor Rachael Hicks, designer Yaffa Jaskoll for the stunning cover, and Lindsay Walter, copyeditor extraordinaire.

And of course, my family. Thank you, Martha, for listening to plot problems and helping to solve them, Gary for making dinner and saying, "Get back to work!" and my boys for enthusiasm, understanding, and patience.

And Mom. Thanks for believing in me.

# About the Author

Katherine Longshore is a former travel agent, coffeehouse barista, and preschool teacher who has finally found her calling writing novels for teens. She is also the author of a series of novels set in the court of Henry VIII, including *Gilt* and *Tarnish*. After five years exploring castles and country manors in England, she now lives in California with three British citizens and one expatriate dog. Visit her online at www.katherinelongshore.com.